LUCY DANIELS

Pigs
— *at the* —
Picnic

Illustrations by Ann Baum

Hodder Children's Books

a division of Hodder Headline plc

Special thanks to Susan Bentley.

**Thanks also to C. J. Hall, B.Vet.Med., M.R.C.V.S., for reviewing
the veterinary information contained in this book.**

Text copyright © 1999 Ben M. Baglio
Created by Ben M. Baglio, London W12 7QY
Illustrations copyright © 1999 Ann Baum

First published in Great Britain in 1999
by Hodder Children's Books

A Catalogue record for this book is available from the British Library

ISBN 0 340 73599 6

Typeset by Avon Dataset Ltd, Bidford-on-Avon, Warks

Printed and bound in Great Britain by
Clays Ltd, St Ives plc

Hodder Children's Books
a division of Hodder Headline plc
338 Euston Road
London NW1 3BH

One

'We must be almost there now,' Mandy Hope said excitedly. 'Two whole weeks on a working farm! It's got to be the most brilliant prize ever!'

Mandy's dad grinned at her in the driving mirror. 'It's certainly yours and James's dream prize! But it sounds like a lot of hard work to me. Are you sure you two are up to it?'

Mandy grinned back. 'Piece of cake! We'll love it, won't we, James?'

'You bet!' James replied. James Hunter was Mandy's best friend. They went to the same school in Walton, where James was in the year below her. They hadn't needed any encouragement from their class teachers to enter the regional competition to create an environmentally-friendly school scheme. They had worked jointly on their winning entry.

Mandy fished a crumpled piece of glossy paper out of her jeans pocket. She smoothed out the brochure, which had *Countryside Trust Working Holidays* printed across the top. 'It says here that all the farms are dedicated to preserving traditional farming methods,' she said.

'That's right,' Mr Hope said. 'The Countryside Trust's a big organisation which owns a lot of farms. Competitions like this one mean that kids get a holiday and the farms benefit from the extra help.'

Emily Hope, Mandy's mum, chuckled. She pushed a strand of red hair away from her face. 'I'm surprised that brochure has any print left on it, the number of times Mandy and James have read it.'

Everyone laughed. James, shy as usual, blushed and adjusted his glasses.

'You know, farm work's very character-building,' Mr Hope commented. 'Getting up at daybreak. Helping with the milking before breakfast. And then there's all the lovely mucking out. Not to mention scrubbing out feed buckets. You'll have done a day's work by mid-morning . . .'

'Oh, ha-ha.' Mandy was used to her dad's teasing. She leaned over his shoulder and looked out of the windscreen as the Land-rover bumped down the stony track.

The cluster of stone buildings was now visible through the trees; summer sunlight gleamed on the slate roofs. Five Acre Farm, where Mandy and James were to spend their working holiday, nestled in the bottom of a narrow valley, overlooked by one of the highest peaks in Yorkshire.

As Mr Hope steered the Land-rover through the farm gate and into the farmyard, Mandy just had time to glimpse the paddock on their right. She dug James in the ribs and they both craned their necks for a brief glance at a huge horse that was grazing placidly beneath some trees. Its coat was a warm, rich chestnut.

'Oh,' Mandy breathed, 'isn't it beautiful? I wonder what breed it is.'

'Looks like a Suffolk Punch,' Mr Hope said, as he drew the Land-rover to a halt and everyone began piling out.

Mandy saw a woman come out of one of the farm buildings and walk towards them.

'Hi there,' the woman said, with a friendly smile, shielding her face from the sun with one hand. Her long brown hair was held back with a white hair-band and she wore a huge white apron over a T-shirt and jeans. 'Excuse the get-up. I've been working in the dairy. I'm Karen Capthorne. Call me Karen, everyone does.'

She shook hands with Mr and Mrs Hope, then turned to Mandy and James. 'Welcome to Five Acre Farm. Come on into the farmhouse. I'll show you where to put your things, then I expect your mum and dad would like a cup of tea. I know I could do with one.'

'She's nice, isn't she?' James said to Mandy, as they lugged their suitcases into the house.

Upstairs Karen showed them to their bedrooms, explaining that they'd be sharing with other young volunteers. She checked her list. 'Mandy, you'll be sharing with Jill Righton. And James, you'll be with Daniel Shaw. They'll be here this afternoon. The volunteers that have already arrived are in the three rooms down the hall – you'll meet them later. Well – I'll leave you to get unpacked. Come on down to the kitchen when you're ready. My husband, Tom, will be in soon for his breakfast.'

'Breakfast?' James whispered, as Karen went downstairs. 'It's a bit late for that, isn't it? It's halfway to lunch-time!'

Mandy chuckled. 'Dad wasn't joking when he said farmers get up at daybreak and do a full day's work before they sit down to eat. I bet we'll be expected to do the same.'

'Oh.' James looked a bit worried. 'I suppose it is only for two weeks.' He went off to his bedroom to unpack his case.

Mandy chuckled to herself. James had what her gran, Dorothy Hope, called 'a very healthy appetite'.

It took Mandy only a few minutes to put her clothes away. She put her pyjamas on one of the beds, slid her empty case under it, then went to the window. Leaning her elbows on the deep stone sill, she gazed out at the view and gave a big sigh of contentment.

Against the ribbed background of limestone-scarred hills, Five Acre Farm was spread out like a patchwork rug. Across the yard, Mandy could see the paddock with the big chestnut horse and, farther away, the pastures.

There were cows grazing in a field, each of them dark brown with a broad white stripe along its back and a pure white tail. Grazing happily alongside were different kinds of sheep. Mandy opened the bedroom window and poked her head out so she could see further. To her right, she saw oblongs of fields with their crops in all shades of green and gold. The orchard, with its beehives, was over to her left and beyond that she could see the glint of a pond.

James came dashing along the landing just as she

came out of the bedroom. 'Have you looked out of your window?' he said. 'This place is great!'

'I know,' Mandy said excitedly. 'I've already seen a few of the animals.'

James pushed his glasses up his nose. 'This is going to be a brilliant holiday!'

The enormous farmhouse kitchen was cool and welcoming. Faded blue wooden shutters hung at the windows and a bright-red Aga contrasted with the grey stone walls. A huge wooden table and chairs took up one part of the room; a number of battered, but comfy-looking easy chairs took up another.

Mandy's mum and dad were just finishing their tea. There was a man sitting at the table with them. He turned and smiled.

'Hello. I'm Tom. Pleased to meet you both.' He had sandy hair and a face full of freckles. His blue eyes crinkled at the corners when he smiled.

'Hi,' Mandy and James replied, smiling back.

Karen came over and placed an enormous plateful of food in front of her husband. 'Your mum and dad have been telling us all about Animal Ark,' she said to Mandy. 'Apparently you help out in the surgery?'

Mandy nodded. 'As much as I can. I'm going to be a vet too, one day.'

'Could be very useful, having someone around who knows a bit about animals,' Tom said, through a mouthful of sausage. 'Some of the volunteers we've had here haven't known one end of a cow from the other.'

Everyone laughed.

'I expect they knew which end to milk by the end of their two weeks!' Mr Hope said. 'You'll have no problem with these two. If it's got fur or feathers, it'll be an instant hit. As for people – that's another matter . . .'

Mandy rolled her eyes at James. Her dad could be so embarrassing sometimes.

'Thanks for the tea, Karen,' Mrs Hope said after a few minutes. 'I think we'd better be making tracks, Adam.'

In the yard Mandy gave her mum and dad a hug. 'Remember to give Flopsy, Mopsy and Cottontail a hug for me.' They were her three pet rabbits.

'We will, love.' Mrs Hope gave Mandy a warm smile.

'Bye, Mr and Mrs Hope,' James said. 'Thanks for bringing me.'

'A pleasure, James,' Mr Hope said. 'Have fun, you two. We'll see you both here the weekend after next.'

Mandy's parents were going back home to Welford now, but were returning for a weekend break in two weeks' time. They would be staying in the nearby village, then picking up Mandy and James on their way back home.

'We're having a fund-raising event here that weekend,' Karen said. 'On the Sunday, in fact. The farm's going to be open to visitors and sponsors and there'll be music and an open-air picnic. Why don't you come along?'

'Sounds wonderful,' Mr Hope said. 'Thanks. We'd be glad to come.'

Mandy and James waved as Mr and Mrs Hope drove off, then they turned to Karen, who was waiting nearby. 'OK, you two. Ready for the grand tour? I usually start with the home acre.'

'Home acre?' James said.

'It's what we call the area around the farmyard,' Karen explained, pointing out the various farm buildings, the kitchen garden and the orchard. 'Come on, I'll show you the dairy. You'll usually find me in there, if I'm not in the office up to my ears in paperwork.'

They reached the dairy and went inside. Mandy and James looked round at the spotless tiled floor, deep sinks, and butter and cheese making equipment.

'Will we get the chance to work in here with you?' Mandy asked.

'If you like.' Karen smiled. 'We encourage our volunteers to have a go at everything.'

James eyed a heavy-looking metal press which stood on the floor. 'What's this for?'

'Pressing cheese,' Karen replied. 'That metal tank over there's the cheese vat. And the thing that looks a bit like a food mixer's a cream separator.'

'I didn't think there'd be so much equipment,' Mandy said. 'Cheese making looks really complicated.'

Karen laughed. 'I suppose it is, until you know what you're doing. Making butter isn't all that difficult. You can have a go at that sometime.'

Karen's tour moved on past the orchard, where the trees were heavy with apples and bees buzzed round the wild flowers in the grass. Mandy heard a muted drone coming from a row of beehives as she passed by. The kitchen garden, with its neat rows of vegetables and wigwams of runner beans, was at the back of the farmhouse.

'This is a bit like your grandad's garden at Lilac Cottage,' James said to Mandy. Adam's parents, Tom and Dorothy Hope, also lived in Welford.

Back in the yard, Karen pushed open the door of an empty barn. 'I've got plans for this place,' she confided. 'I want to enlarge the farm shop. We open on Sunday mornings at present and sell our own butter, cheese and honey. I think we could do well if we sold a bigger range of goods and opened a few more days a week.'

'That's great idea, isn't it, James?' Mandy said.

James nodded.

Karen grinned. 'Glad you think so. The building work is going to be costly. I just hope the sponsors will be generous at our fund-raising event. They agree to the idea in principle, but there's only so much money to go round and Five Acre isn't the only farm owned by the Trust.'

Mandy saw a shadow pass over Karen's face. For a moment the farm manager looked worried, then her face cleared. 'Right then. Come on, you two,' she said. 'There's just the cowshed left to see.'

Inside the cosy shed, Mandy and James looked round. There was a manger against one wall and a deep layer of straw and bracken on the floor. 'Do the cows sleep in here every night?' James asked.

'No,' Karen shook her head. 'In the summer they want to stay out and eat grass. We don't feed them then, except for a kilo or two of rolled barley to keep them contented. But in the winter they're eager to come in, because the grass isn't so good and they're hungry.'

Apart from a churn in one corner, Mandy couldn't see any other machinery. 'Where do you keep your milking equipment?' she asked.

'Right here.' Karen waggled her fingers. 'You're looking at it!'

'Oh!' Mandy laughed. 'Of course.'

'We milk our cows by hand twice a day,' Karen explained. 'First thing in the morning and again in the evening.'

'I saw your cows from my bedroom window,' Mandy said eagerly. 'And you've got lots of different breeds of pigs too, haven't you? Can we go and see them, please?' Barns and cowsheds were very interesting, but she was itching to go and find out about the animals.

'Sure,' Karen said. 'The boring bit's over with anyway.'

Mandy felt herself blush. 'Oh, I didn't mean that.'

'That's all right,' Karen said good-naturedly.

'There was a huge chestnut horse in the paddock on the way in,' James put in hopefully. 'I wouldn't mind having a look at her.'

Karen chuckled. 'That's Hazel, our Suffolk Punch. She's quite a character.' She pointed towards the pastures. 'Take the short cut by the orchard. You'll find Pete Brady over there. He's our stockman. He'll show you the animals. What he doesn't know about animals you could fit on a postage stamp.'

'Right!' Mandy and James didn't need telling

twice. They hurried across the yard and cut down the path by the side of the orchard.

Over at the pastures, Mandy and James saw a man clearing grass from a cattle trough.

'That must be Pete Brady,' Mandy said.

Straightening up, the man peered short-sightedly at Mandy and James as they came towards him. Despite the hot weather, he wore a tweed cap and dark-blue overalls. His face was lined and deeply tanned.

'Now then. I take it you're going to be helping out round here for the next couple of weeks?' he greeted them, blunt and to the point.

Mandy and James nodded. 'Karen said you'd show us the animals, Mr Brady,' Mandy said.

'Did she now?' Mr Brady said, rubbing the heel of his hand across his bristly chin. 'It's lucky I've just finished here, then, and I'm about to go on my rounds. Come on, can't stand here dilly-dallying all day.' He stomped off across the field.

'He's not very friendly, is he?' James whispered to Mandy.

She shrugged. 'Maybe he likes animals more than people!'

The small herd of cattle looked up with mild brown eyes as Mandy, James and Mr Brady approached. Their white tails swished back and forth, brushing away the files.

'Aren't they lovely?' Mandy breathed. 'What kind are they?'

'Gloucesters – a breed with a long history,' Mr Brady said, shortly. 'Ours is one of the few remaining herds in the country.'

'Really?' Mandy said.

'Oh, aye,' came the reply. 'They've won lots of prizes at county shows. Their calves fetch a good price too. Tom and Karen sell them on for breeding.'

Mandy and James had barely spent a few minutes admiring the chocolate-brown and white cows before Mr Brady suddenly turned on his heel and marched off. 'Come away, then,' he called over his shoulder. 'I told you. I've got my rounds to do.'

Mandy stifled a giggle as they set off after Mr Brady's stooped figure. They had to stride out to keep up with him as he went back through the orchard and led them past the duckpond.

'Where's he off to now?' Mandy whispered.

'Looks like we're heading towards the woods,' James answered.

'Aye.' Mr Brady suddenly spoke up. 'That's where we keep the pigs. I've been having to keep a close eye on two new arrivals.'

Mandy and James exchanged glances. There was nothing wrong with Pete Brady's hearing!

'This wooden fence marks the boundary of Five Acre,' the stockman informed them as he unfastened a gate and led the way into the woods. He pointed across to some fields of crops and a complex of low, modern farm buildings. 'That's Nixon Manor Farm over there. We don't have a lot to do with them.'

'Why not?' Mandy asked politely.

'Jim Nixon's got his ideas about farming and we've got ours,' Mr Brady muttered.

'And they don't match up?' James asked.

'That's right,' came the gruff reply. 'The two farms are like chalk and cheese.'

Mandy and James looked beyond the trees to where a tractor, pulling a trailer, was beetling its way up and down the nearest field. A fine mist hung over the area behind the trailer and there was a chemical smell in the air.

Mandy was curious about Nixon Manor and would have liked to find out more, but just then she spotted a number of pigs. They were rooting around contentedly in the cool beneath the trees.

'Oh!' she said delightedly. 'Just look at them all. What breed are those?' She pointed to some pigs with black, compact bodies. They had short faces with white turned-up snouts.

'You two like pigs?' Pete asked, his chin coming up.

'Oh, yes,' Mandy said. 'We love them, don't we, James?'

James nodded. 'We helped a schoolmate of ours, Brandon Gill, look after Ruby at Greystones Farm.'

'Ruby was the runt of the litter,' Mandy explained. 'But she grew into a big, beautiful pig.'

'A British Saddleback,' James added.

Pete had been listening intently. Now he gave Mandy and James a gap-toothed grin, his eyes twinkling. 'We've three different breeds of pig at Five Acre – or rather four now, counting the new arrivals. These black ones are Berkshires. And those over there are Middle Whites. See? Both breeds have thick-set bodies and flat dish-faces.'

'What are those pink pigs with the black spots on them, over by the oak tree?' asked James. 'Crikey! Haven't they got big floppy ears!'

'Gloucester Old Spots,' Mr Brady said proudly. 'Lovely pigs. Very docile. They don't stray far – their ears stop them seeing too far ahead.'

Suddenly there was a terrific banging noise. Mandy whirled round. She noticed for the first time that there was a large pen, made of sheets of corrugated iron, set back amongst the trees. It sounded as if someone was attacking the metal walls with hammers. There came a sudden squeal of piggy rage.

'Oh, blimey,' Mr Brady said, with a chuckle. 'They're at it again.' Springing into action, he went stamping off towards the pen.

'What's in there? Super-pig?' James joked.

He and Mandy dashed after the stockman.

'Stop that, you blighters!' Mr Brady cried as he reached the pen.

The banging noise stopped for an instant, then there was a renewed scrabbling on metal that set Mandy's teeth on edge. Suddenly a long snout and two pricked ears appeared as a pig stood up on its hind legs.

Mr Brady pushed his cap to the back of his head. 'Meet Copper!' he said.

'Wow!' James gasped.

Mandy stared back in utter amazement. The pig was covered with a thick coat of fox-red hair. It looked more like a small bear than a pig. She had never seen anything like it!

Two

As Copper thrust his head towards Mandy, she gave a breathless little laugh and leaned back.

'He's huge!' she said. 'And his mate's not much smaller. What's her name, Mr Brady?'

'Comet,' came the prompt answer. 'Lovely, isn't she?'

'They both are,' James replied. 'What breed are they?'

'Tamworths,' Mr Brady said, beaming with pride. 'A really old breed, not too far removed from a wild boar.'

'Really?' Mandy said, her eyes widening.

'Oh, aye. We're lucky to have them. They're on the rare and endangered list. That's about as rare as an animal gets before it becomes extinct.'

'Wow!' James said. 'But they're not endangered on Five Acre.'

'I should say not, lad,' Mr Brady said, a mysterious twinkle in his eye.

Mandy frowned, wondering what the stockman meant. Then she caught a movement in the doorway of the pig house. 'Oh!' she exclaimed delightedly. 'They've got piglets!'

'That's right,' Pete Brady said. 'Two of them. They're a bit shy. They haven't settled in yet.'

One of the piglets ventured out. It saw Mandy and James and gave a startled oink before it darted straight back inside. Mandy had the briefest glimpse of a tiny pink face, neat trotters and podgy hindquarters.

'Oh, it's adorable!' she cried. 'How old are the piglets? And what are they called?'

'One question at a time, lass!' Mr Brady said, but he looked pleased. 'They're seven weeks old. Two little females – Ginger and Spice.'

Mandy could hardly wait to get a good look at them. She hoped Ginger and Spice would soon be bold enough to come outside. *That shouldn't take long if they take after their cheeky parents*, she thought.

Leaning on her elbows beside James, she looked down into the pen, where Copper was now careering around, hotly pursued by his mate. Comet was determined not to let him get away. She squealed with excitement as she nipped at Copper's muscular hindquarters.

'She won't hurt him, will she?' James said worriedly.

'Nay,' Pete gave a short laugh. 'Those are play bites.'

Suddenly Copper turned the tables on Comet. He whipped round and came to a full stop, so that the other pig was brought up short. Then he grunted and lunged forward. Comet squealed as if her very life was at stake, then set off at top speed round the pen. Now it was Copper's turn to do the chasing!

Mandy, James and Mr Brady burst out laughing. When she could catch her breath again Mandy asked, 'Why do these have to stay in a pen when the other pigs are allowed to roam about, Mr Brady?'

'Oh, these'll be allowed out too, in a week or so,' Mr Brady replied. 'We keep new arrivals by themselves for a while. Just in case they get sick. We wouldn't want any infection to spread to our other animals.'

'Oh, right.' Mandy nodded. She knew all about quarantine. 'At Animal Ark, animals stay in the residential unit if they're too sick to go home,' she said. 'The surgery has a separate area behind the unit for wild or infectious animals.'

'Animal Ark?' Mr Brady looked puzzled for a moment. 'Oh, you're the vets' daughter. Karen said one of our helpers was animal mad.'

'That's Mandy all right!' James said. Mandy dug him in the ribs. 'Look who's talking!'

The stockman gave another toothy grin. He was a different person now, his former grumpiness forgotten. Obviously, anyone who liked pigs was all right with him.

'You can do away with the "Mr Brady",' he said. 'Call me Pete, right?'

'OK,' Mandy and James replied.

'You know. There's nowt to beat Tamworths in my opinion,' Pete enthused, watching Copper and Comet rooting round their pen. 'That hairy red coat protects them from sunburn, so they can live where it's hot and humid. But I've heard of them living outdoors up in northern Scotland too. And they're dead smart. You can teach these in ten days what you'd take ten weeks to teach a dog.'

'Maybe Copper and Comet could give Blackie lessons!' Mandy joked.

'Who's Blackie?' Pete asked.

'My Labrador,' James said with a grin. 'He's lovely but he's not exactly obedient.'

Mandy frowned thoughtfully. 'Copper's name really suits him – he's copper-coloured. But why's the other pig called Comet?'

'If she ever gets out and takes off across the fields, you'll find out!' Pete joked. 'We had a real job to get her into this pen. I've never seen a pig run so fast. I reckon Comet could take on a greyhound and win!'

Comet gave a throaty grunt and nodded her head up and down, as if she agreed with every word Pete had said. Mandy and James chuckled. These pigs were real characters!

Copper seemed to have tired of the game of tag. He ambled towards the side of the pen, nose held high, snuffling.

'Hey – I've just remembered. The Gills' pigs liked having their backs scratched, didn't they?' Mandy said. She found a strong twig lying on the ground and leaned over carefully to show it to Copper.

He stayed his ground, so she began scratching his hairy side. Copper pushed up harder against the stick, leaning against the wall. He closed his eyes and grunted with contentment. One of his back legs pedalled in the air as Mandy's stick scratched a sensitive place on his rump.

'He really loves that,' James said with a chuckle.

Comet came trotting over, looking with interest at Copper, who was flexing his shoulders and

rubbing up against Mandy's stick. She nudged him with a solid shoulder.

'Do you want a good scratch as well?' James said, picking up a twig.

A moment later, both pigs looked as though they thought they were in heaven.

Mandy and James spent the next half hour helping Pete muck out the pigpen and fill the water trough. Ginger and Spice scurried about, squealing in alarm and darting for shelter as they worked. But when Comet lay on her side, they settled down to feed from her.

'Oh, look,' Mandy whispered, smiling at the piglets, little grunts of contentment. 'Ginger and Spice are getting used to us already.'

While Comet fed her hungry babies, Mandy and James gathered handfuls of grass, weeds and twigs and threw them into the pen.

'I fed them earlier on,' Pete explained. 'This stuff's just for them to root around in. Stops them getting bored, see? I'll be popping down here again after supper. You can come with me if you like.'

'We'd love to, wouldn't we, James?' Mandy said.

James nodded.

'Well – I'd best get on with my rounds,' Pete said, moving away from the pen. 'Got to see if the ducks have laid any eggs. They lay them anywhere – in the muddy water, on the edge of the pond. Eggs left lying around get contaminated and then they're dangerous to eat . . .'

Rather reluctantly, Mandy and James fell into step with Pete. They would have been happy spending all morning at the pigpen, waiting for the piglets to put in another appearance.

'See you later, Copper and Comet,' Mandy said. 'And you, Ginger and Spice.'

'Time for lunch,' Pete announced a couple of hours later. 'Everyone meets up in the farmhouse kitchen at mealtimes. We'd best go in and clean up.'

As Mandy, James and Pete went into the kitchen, Karen looked up and flashed them a smile. 'Hello, you two. Has Pete been keeping you busy?'

'Yes. But we loved it,' Mandy said. 'Especially helping with the pigs. Copper and Comet's babies are gorgeous, aren't they, James?'

James nodded.

'They are rather special,' Karen agreed. 'Come and meet the rest of the team. And your room-mates are here now. That's Jill over there and Daniel's next to Tom.'

Mandy saw a tall, thin girl with very short brown hair. 'Hi, Jill,' she said. 'I'm Mandy. Have you just arrived? You're going to love it here.'

'You think so?' Jill mumbled. 'I don't even *want* to be here. My parents forced me to come.' She sauntered over to the table and flopped into a seat.

Mandy felt herself flush at the girl's rudeness. She hoped Jill would be more friendly once she got to know her better.

Over at the table, she saw that James seemed to have forgotten his usual shyness. He was talking to a boy with spiky hair and a round, open face. She went over and sat next to them.

'This is Mandy,' James introduced her to his room-mate. 'She's my best friend. We both live in Welford village, not too far from here.'

'Hi, Mandy. Isn't this great?' Daniel said. 'I've never been on a farm before.'

Mandy smiled, liking Daniel at once. Just then, Tom spoke up. He had rolled up his shirt sleeves and was cutting slices from a crusty brown loaf. 'Fetch plates from the dresser, everyone, and help yourself to food,' he said cheerfully. 'We don't stand on ceremony here.'

Mandy, James and the other volunteers piled their plates with salads, cheese, pickles and bread. Mandy thought the kitchen seemed a lot smaller with so many people inside. The air was buzzing with introductions and excited chatter.

She saw that her room-mate was staring out of

the window, shoulders hunched and her chin propped on her hand. 'I wonder if I should go over and try to talk to Jill,' she said to James.

James took one look at the sulky girl. 'I wouldn't bother,' he said.

Mandy shrugged. 'Maybe you're right. She looks like she'd rather be left alone.'

After the meal, Mandy and James washed up, while the others cleared the table and put away the crockery.

'Right, listen up everyone,' Karen said brightly, once everything was neat and tidy. 'Jobs for this afternoon. Jill and Daniel, you'll be over at Hazel's paddock. Mandy and James, you'll be helping Tom with hedge clearing . . .'

Outside in the yard, James rolled his eyes. 'Oh, good. Hedge clearing!'

Mandy chuckled. 'Think of it as a challenge. Come on. I'll race you!'

'You're on!' James was already darting for the fields.

A couple of minutes later, they reached the hedgerow.

'I admire your eagerness, I must say!' Tom joked, arriving just as they had regained their breath. He handed them each a rake. 'Here you go. As I cut these branches, you two can rake them into a pile.'

He began clearing the base of an overgrown hedge with a short curved blade fitted to a wooden handle.

'What's that tool called?' James wanted to know.

'A bagging hook,' Tom said. 'And very dangerous it is too. You could easily lose a finger or thumb.' He showed them how he was holding back weeds with a stick, as he swung the hook back and forth.

An hour later, the hedge had been trimmed and the branches and weeds dealt with. Tom wiped his forehead with his handkerchief. 'Phew. That's a good job done. Fancy coming into the village with me? I need to buy some fence wire.'

Mandy and James nodded. 'OK.'

They called into the farmhouse to tell Karen where they were going, then piled into the Land-rover. Mandy and James looked out of the car window at the narrow roads, flanked on both sides by dry-stone walls. The dales were beautiful in the summer sun, from the gentle green slopes of the hillside to the miles of limestone pavement that formed terraces up on the high slopes.

'Grand, isn't it?' Tom said. 'Best scenery in the world.'

Mandy and James agreed. They loved living in Yorkshire.

Holtwick, with its square church tower and rows

of stone cottages, soon came into view. As Tom drove down the high street, he pointed to a cottage that stood back from the road. 'Pete Brady lives there with his mother. He cycles over to Five Acre every day.'

Mandy looked at James. They had a job keeping straight faces. Pete Brady's mother must be about a hundred and ten!

'He's probably not as old as he looks,' Mandy whispered. 'Working outdoors makes your skin all weathered and leathery like that.'

Tom parked the Land-rover opposite a row of shops. The farm suppliers was a general store, housed in a converted barn of grey Yorkshire stone.

'That barn's similar to the one at Five Acre,' James said. 'The one Karen wants to use to extend the farm shop.'

'Told you two about that, did she?' Tom said with a smile. 'Karen's got ambitions for Five Acre. This fund-raising event's very important to her.'

Inside the shop, Mandy saw that there were only two other customers, a tall man with greying dark hair and a lanky, dark-haired boy, wearing a checked shirt. The family resemblance was striking. Mandy guessed they were father and son.

Tom nodded a greeting to them both. 'Afternoon, Jim. Hello, Neil,' he said brightly.

The man nodded briefly, but Mandy noticed that the boy gave Tom a hostile look.

'I'll be a minute sorting out this wire,' Tom said. 'Why don't you two have a look round?'

'OK,' Mandy replied, moving away. 'I wonder if they sell postcards. I might send one to Mum and Dad.'

'Good idea,' James said.

They wandered towards a rack of cards which was near a display of fruit and vegetables. Mandy had just decided on a card with a picture of two Shire horses when Tom walked past, a roll of fence wire under his arm.

'Ah, Tom. I'm glad you looked in,' came the voice of the shopkeeper. 'I was about to ring Five Acre and order some more of your fruit and veg. The last lot was snapped up. Organic produce seems to be getting really popular round here.'

Mandy found herself listening to the conversation. Anything to do with Five Acre interested her.

'Glad to hear it,' Tom was saying to the shopkeeper. 'But I'm not that surprised. People are catching on that it tastes better, besides being free from chemicals.'

'I reckon you're right there,' the other man said. 'It's the same with all the shops round here. Sales of organic produce are way up.'

'The customer's always right, eh?' Tom said, handing over some money.

'What utter rubbish!' grumbled a loud voice beside Mandy. 'In my book, a carrot's a carrot, no matter how it's grown. At Nixon Manor we've been using the same growing methods for donkey's years. Organic farming's just the latest fashion.'

'I can't agree with you there, Jim, I'm afraid,' Tom said good-naturedly.

Mandy turned round. The other man was looking in Tom's direction, a worried look on his face despite his challenging words.

The dark-haired boy was standing close to his father, shoulders squared and chin set defensively. He glowered at Tom from under straight black brows. 'Our crops are top quality,' he said. 'We don't need any gimmicks to sell them!'

'You and I know that, Neil,' his father said. 'And our customers have always been satisfied. But some farmers around here have jumped-up ideas.'

'I'm sorry you feel that way,' Tom said. 'Maybe you should drop in at Five Acre sometime. I reckon we have more in common than you think.'

Jim Nixon snorted dismissively. 'I doubt it! Come on, Neil,' he snapped. 'I've no more time to waste. We'll pick up our supplies later.'

Turning on his heel, the farmer stalked away. Neil

followed his father without a backward glance, his hands thrust into his jeans pockets.

Tom was waiting at the checkout when Mandy and James went to pay for their postcards. 'As you heard,' he said with a wry smile, 'our neighbours aren't exactly friendly.'

'No,' James agreed. 'Mr Nixon and Neil seem dead against organic farming.'

Tom stroked his chin. 'To be honest, I doubt Jim Nixon knows very much about our methods. He's the type who'd condemn a thing without finding out the facts. Neil's bound to go along with anything his father says.'

'I wonder why Mr Nixon looked worried,' Mandy commented, thoughtfully.

'It could be he's feeling a bit threatened by our success,' Tom said. 'Jim's used to supplying the shops and local businesses with his produce. Our sales might only be a drop in the ocean to a big farmer like him, but I don't imagine he takes kindly to anyone cutting into his profits.'

Three

On their return to Five Acre, Mandy and James spent the next couple of hours helping Tom mend a stretch of wire fence.

'Isn't it suppertime yet?' James whispered to Mandy. 'I'm starving hungry!'

She grinned at him. 'It's farm work. It gives you a huge appetite.'

'Right, finished,' Tom said, a few minutes later. He began gathering up his tools. 'Thanks for your help, you two. Why don't you go into the house? Supper will be ready soon. That ought to please you, James!'

James reddened. 'Er . . . yes,' he murmured.

As Mandy went upstairs to wash, she noticed that

her bedroom door was open. She glanced inside and saw Jill lying stretched out on her bed, reading a magazine.

'Hi, Jill,' Mandy said. 'Are you coming downstairs?'

Jill looked up, her pale face unfriendly. 'Why, what's happening?'

'We're just about to have supper,' Mandy said.

Jill went back to reading her magazine. 'Big deal,' she muttered.

Mandy looked at the miserable, sulky girl and her heart sank. Two weeks sharing a bedroom with her didn't look like being much fun.

She went to the bathroom and washed her hands. On her way down to the kitchen she bumped into James. He was with Daniel and they were laughing and chatting. 'Hi, you two,' Mandy said, wishing her room-mate was as easy-going.

Just before the meal started, Mandy noticed Jill slip into the room and take her place at the other end of the table. She sighed, wondering why the girl was so difficult.

Supper was a hot pasta dish with lots of salads and fresh bread. It was noisy in the kitchen, with farm workers and volunteers chatting about the day's events.

After a dessert of apple pie and cream, everyone took their plates to the sink.

'Right then,' Karen said to Mandy and James. 'Since you've taken such a shine to our pigs, I'm going to introduce you to the high art of the pig bucket!' Grinning at their blank faces, she opened a cupboard beneath the sink.

'We put all the household scraps into this bucket,' she explained. 'Then, before we wash up, we scrape the plates clean and dribble hot water over them to wash any leftovers into a bowl. This first washing-up water gets tipped into the pig bucket too. When you only keep a few pigs, the pig bucket's a valuable source of extra nutrients.'

Mandy and James rinsed all the plates as Karen had shown them, before washing them in the usual way. Then they put the bucket by the back door, ready to be taken down to the pigpen.

Just as everyone had finished clearing up, Pete Brady came to the back door. 'I'm just going down to the woods to check on them pigs before I get off home. Anyone want to come?'

'Yep!' Mandy said. 'We're ready, aren't we, James?'

James nodded, heading for the door. 'Pig bucket and all!'

'I'll come too,' Daniel said. 'I haven't been down there yet.'

James and Daniel carried the brimming pig bucket between them. On reaching the woods, they closed the gate behind them, before walking through the trees.

Pete bent down to pick up a stick, then he turned to James and Daniel. 'Make sure you keep that bucket held up,' he said, with a twinkle in his eye. 'Here you go, Mandy, lass. Bang this stick against that bucket.'

'OK.' Mandy wondered what the stockman was up to, but she raised her arm. The metallic clanging echoed through the trees.

'Crikey!' James said, as all the different pigs came hurrying towards them. It was a pig stampede. Black pigs, white pigs, and spotted pigs all came trotting,

heads down, grunting excitedly.

Daniel looked alarmed. 'They don't attack people, do they?'

Pete shook his head. 'Nay, lad. Pigs are easy-going animals – just so long as you treat them right.'

As they drew near Copper's and Comet's pen, there was a familiar scrabbling on metal, and excited squealing and grunting. Two sandy trotters appeared, then Copper's cheeky snout and finally his head appeared above the metal wall. A few seconds later, another head appeared. Comet! The two pigs were side by side, looking over the pen, ears pricked intelligently, noses snuffling up the delicious smells coming from the pig bucket.

'Uh-oh!' Mandy said, stifling a giggle. 'I think they want to join in!'

She craned her neck, looking towards the pig house. Would Ginger and Spice be feeling secure enough to explore their new home?

'Yes!' she cried, as two piglets exploded from the doorway. They began darting nimbly back and forth between their massive parents' feet.

'Ah!' Daniel crooned, as he spotted them.

Pete took the bucket and let himself into the pen. He tipped some scraps into the trough. 'Copper and Comet and their babies get a good portion of this. They need the extra vitamins while they're cooped up. Once they get outside, like this lot, they'll get a lot of their nourishment from rooting about.'

'Wow!' Daniel seemed spellbound by the pigs. Pete had tipped out the remains of the bucket and they were snuffling around and jostling each other to get their fair share. 'These are amazing! Look at those spotted ones and those black ones with squashed noses! I've only ever seen pink ones. And that was on TV!'

'Haven't you ever seen a live pig before?' Mandy said. It seemed really strange to her. She had been surrounded by animals her whole life.

Daniel shook his head. 'I live in the centre of Northampton. There are plenty of cats and dogs, but not farm animals! That's why I wanted to come and work on Five Acre. I love animals, but I don't know much about many of them.'

'Well, there's loads of animals here to make friends with!' Mandy said.

'Too right!' Daniel's eyes lit up. 'I'm dead glad I came!'

By the time they headed back to the farmhouse, the sky was streaked with orange and crimson. Long purple shadows lay over the fields. Daniel was asking Pete Brady a constant stream of questions. What did pigs eat? How long did they live?

'He's got pigs on the brain!' James said with a grin.

Mandy chuckled. 'Wouldn't you have? If you had never seen one, then you got to meet loads of them all at once. *And* the most brilliant pigs ever!'

Back at the farmyard, Pete fetched his rickety old bike from the barn. Mandy, James and Daniel waved as the stockman cycled up the stony track that led to the Holtwick road. When he had gone, they went inside the farmhouse.

In the kitchen, Tom was sitting at the table, a pile of paperwork in front of him. Mandy saw that all the easy chairs were occupied by various volunteers who were playing computer games, reading, or just chatting.

'Where's Karen, Tom?' Mandy asked.

'In the office, working,' he replied. 'She's sending the sponsors individual letters. It's less than two weeks before the farm's fund-raising open day.'

Just then the office door opened, and Karen came out carrying a bundle of envelopes. She put them on a shelf in the kitchen. 'So I'll remember to post them tomorrow,' she explained.

'Right, you lot.' Tom suddenly jumped up. 'Enough of this lounging around. Who fancies a bit of a sing-song?'

Mandy saw glances of horror flick between the various young volunteers.

'I don't think so,' Jill sneered.

Mandy felt torn. She liked Tom, but she had to admit that a sing-song was a terrible idea.

Undaunted, Tom looked round at the gloomy faces. He seemed to have been expecting this reaction. 'Oh, come on!' he teased, with a rich chuckle. 'Don't knock it until you've tried it.'

'It's an old tradition on Five Acre,' Karen explained, looking amused. 'I'm afraid Tom insists we all join in! And that includes you, Jill.'

Tom fetched a songbook, a couple of guitars and an old tambourine. 'Come on, everyone,' he said, shepherding them into a group. 'Put those cushions on the floor and plonk yourselves down here. Can anyone play the guitar . . .?'

'This is going to be a disaster!' James groaned. 'I bet he starts singing Ging-gang-goolie . . .'

'Don't!' Mandy almost spluttered with embarrassed laughter. Singing wasn't her strong point. Her dad was the talented one in the family; he sang in the Welford church choir.

'Here we go!' Tom strummed his guitar. He began singing, his rich baritone voice filling the kitchen.

'Hey, that's in the charts,' Mandy said, surprised.

Hesitantly at first, the others began to join in.

They knew the song and liked it. After a struggle, Mandy overcame her reluctance and began to sing. She dug James in the ribs and he joined in, his face bright red.

Suddenly another voice swelled tunefully out over the others, reaching impossible high notes and sending shivers rippling down Mandy's back. Everyone turned in wonder.

Mandy felt her mouth drop open as she saw Jill, her eyes closed, singing for all she was worth. Her voice was sweet, rich, and with a haunting quality.

James's eyes were round behind his glasses. 'Wow!' he breathed. 'She's fantastic!'

The sing-song was transformed. Jill's wonderful voice gave heart to those who were less talented. When Tom put down his guitar, an hour or so later, there were genuine groans of protest.

'Just one more song then,' he said, grinning triumphantly. 'We're harvesting the early wheat tomorrow, so we can't afford a late night. OK, everyone?'

After the strains of the final song had faded, everybody said goodnight and went upstairs. Mandy undressed, then climbed into bed. She lay staring into the darkness. The first day was almost over, and she felt tired but happy.

'Goodnight, Jill,' she whispered sleepily, as

her room-mate climbed into bed.

There was a long pause, before the brief reply, 'Night . . .'

Next morning, Mandy jumped out of bed and opened the curtains. She leaned out of the open window.

The air smelled fresh and sweet, and birdsong rippled on the breeze. The farm was still wreathed in mist and glowing in the sunlight.

Mandy saw a movement over in the wheatfield. 'Oh,' she breathed, captivated by the sight of Hazel, in a horse-collar and full harness, toiling patiently up and down between the shafts of a mower.

Hurriedly, she pulled on a T-shirt and shorts, then stooped to give Jill a gentle shake before heading for the bathroom. 'Uh?' Jill groaned and rubbed her eyes. 'What time is it?'

'Time to go to work!' Mandy called over her shoulder, already dashing out of the room.

She washed, then went to knock on James's bedroom door, just as it opened. James and Daniel came out, both fully dressed.

'Hazel's already working in the wheatfield,' Mandy said excitedly.

'We saw her too,' James said, as they hurried downstairs.

In the kitchen, Karen was pouring tea from an enormous pot. She looked up and smiled. 'Grab a cup,' she said. 'Then it's all out to help with harvesting.'

When Mandy and James had finished their tea they went into the farmyard. They saw a lanky, dark-haired boy walking in through the farm gate.

'Isn't that Neil Nixon?' James said.

Mandy nodded. 'I wonder what he wants.'

'I don't know,' James said, looking a bit nervous. 'But he's coming over.'

Neil came to a halt. 'I saw you yesterday, in Holtwick, didn't I?' he said bluntly, looking down at them. 'So are you two townies then, come to play on the farm, or what?'

Mandy stood her ground. 'Where we live is farming country too,' she said. 'My mum and dad are both vets. So we get to see loads of farm animals.'

'Yeah?' Neil said with a narrow grin. 'You must think yourself quite an animal expert.'

'Not really,' she answered with a shrug. 'But I suppose I know more about them than most people.'

'We're here for a working holiday,' James put in. 'We won it in a competition.'

Neil raised his dark eyebrows. 'Funny sort of prize.'

Just then Karen came out into the yard. 'Hello, Neil,' she said, looking surprised. 'What brings you here?'

Neil shuffled his feet. 'Tom invited me. He said Dad and I should drop in sometime. It's my day off, so I thought I'd come over.' He fixed Mandy and James with defiant blue eyes. 'Go on, tell her. You heard him invite me, yesterday in the shop.'

Mandy searched her memory. 'I think Tom did say something like that . . .'

'Don't worry about it,' Karen said with a friendly smile. 'You're welcome here any time, Neil. Come into the house. The tea's still fresh. Everyone else has gone to help with the harvesting, but I've some paperwork to do. You can keep me company. I'll show you round later, if you like.'

Neil brightened. 'Oh, right. I'd like that. Thanks.' He threw another hard, blue-eyed look over his shoulder at Mandy and James. 'Maybe see you later. Don't work too hard.'

Mandy and James set off for the wheatfield.

'How come Neil's interested in Five Acre all of a sudden?' James said.

'I don't know,' Mandy said thoughtfully. 'But I don't trust him.' In her head was a picture of the look on Neil's face as he glared at Tom in the farm suppliers the day before.

'Ah, here comes more help!' Tom called cheerfully, as they reached the field. 'Right then. Just a few pointers before you start . . .' He explained that a bundle of corn was called a sheaf and each sheaf had to be tied round the middle.

'How much corn makes up a bundle – I mean, sheaf?' James asked, practical as usual.

'Good question,' Tom said. 'Just gather as much as you can handle.'

Mandy and the others set to work. It was dusty, tiring work. By the time Mandy had gathered a sheaf, her clothes were sticking to her. She glanced at James. His cheeks were red and he'd pushed his floppy, dark fringe back from his face.

'Phew! This is hard work,' he said, arms bristling with corn. 'Now what?'

Tom was just coming over. 'Those sheaves look about ready to be tied off. Here's how you do it.' He gripped a sheaf firmly between his knees. Then he rubbed both ends of a handful of corn to make it pliable, looped it round the bundle of stalks, and deftly twisted the two ends together. 'Now – you just tuck the twisted ends under, and that's it!'

The first time Mandy tried to tie her sheaf, it all sprang apart. But at the second go, she got the knack of holding the straw between her knees while she tied it off.

'Well done, Mandy,' Tom beamed. 'You too, James. You did yours first go.'

James blushed. 'Easy as falling off a log!'

At lunch-time, everyone sat in the shade of the hedgerow to eat their picnic of bread, cheese and pickle and fruit – all grown on Five Acre Farm. There was Tom's home-brew or ginger beer to drink.

This is just great, Mandy thought. Sunlight speckled the ground and the warm smell of crushed grass hung over the wheatfield. Hazel stood in the shade of the hedge, tearing at the sweet grass with her strong teeth.

After lunch, the work began again. Soon the field was littered with sheaves. Tom performed another demonstration for Mandy and James and the other volunteers. 'You take two sheaves and bang their heads together – like this. Then you lean four more sheaves against those, and you've got a stook.'

'What does a stook do?' Mandy asked.

'It allows the sun and wind to dry the corn and ripen the grain,' Tom said.

By suppertime all the corn had been gathered and stacked up into stooks. There were dozens and dozens of them. Pete had led Hazel off for a rub-down and a well-earned rest in her paddock. Mandy and James trudged back to the farmhouse with everyone else, tired and dusty but full of satisfaction at a job well done.

Karen was in the kitchen preparing plates of colourful salads, pies and fruit flans. They were surprised to see Neil Nixon sitting at the table. 'We're having a bit of a party,' Karen said over her shoulder. 'It's traditional after the harvest. Neil's joining us. You've all just got time to shower and change.'

'What's he still doing here?' James whispered to Mandy.

'Looks like he's been helping Karen.' Mandy frowned. 'He seemed dead against organic farming yesterday, but now he doesn't seem to want to leave.'

Four

Feeling fresher after her shower, Mandy went outside to the orchard, where the food had been set out on a trestle table.

'Wow!' she said, when she saw the tempting display. Karen had decorated the salads and other dishes with herbs and orange, red and blue flower petals. 'Can you eat those?' she asked.

Karen nodded. 'Lots of flowers are edible. It's just not widely known any more.'

'This looks brilliant!' James said, coming up to the table. His floppy, dark fringe was still damp from the shower.

'I keep telling Karen she ought to do the food for next week's fund-raising,' Tom said, arriving with

Jill, Daniel and the other helpers. 'But she insists on getting outside caterers in.'

Karen chuckled. 'Thanks for the compliment, but I've got enough on my plate already. Besides, the bigwigs who sponsor Five Acre will be expecting something a bit posher than my home cooking!'

Neil had taken a seat near Mandy and James. 'Haven't you got a machine for cutting and gathering your corn?' she heard him ask Tom. 'It seems stupid to harvest by hand if you don't have to.'

Mandy bit her lip. She wondered if Neil meant to sound so rude.

'I can't argue with that,' Tom said genially. 'The thing is, with our small acreage, it's not worth hiring a cumbersome reaper-and-binder. We manage fine with Hazel and the mower and the goodwill of our neighbours. Now that's something you can't hire!'

'I suppose not,' Neil said, thoughtfully. 'But you do use some machinery and stuff here, don't you?'

Karen chuckled. 'Of course we do! Same as you. You've seen our tractors and the modern cooling equipment in the dairy. And I don't know how I'd manage to feed all our workers without the food stored in my freezers.'

Mandy looked at James. Neil seemed to be a bit confused about Five Acre's methods. 'I reckon he thought this place was in a time-warp!' she whispered.

Tom grinned at the older boy. 'Maybe we aren't quite as backward-looking as you thought. Is that it?'

Neil reddened. Tom patted his shoulder. 'It's all right, lad. Your dad's entitled to his opinion. But as I told him, as farmers, we've got more in common than he thinks. Maybe he'd like to come to the fund-raising event? Then he can see for himself.'

'Yeah,' Neil murmured, but he didn't look as if he thought it was likely.

There was the usual laughter and chatter as everyone enjoyed the food. Neil was silent and Mandy noticed that he seemed thoughtful.

At last, James spooned up the final mouthful of his strawberry shortcake and fresh cream. 'I can hardly move,' he groaned, patting his stomach.

'You need a bit of exercise. Come on.' Mandy stood up.

'Where are we going?'

Mandy's eyes lit up. 'I'll give you a clue – two words,' she said, eyeing the left-overs.

'Pig bucket!' James said with a grin.

Karen glanced at Neil. 'Why don't you go with Mandy and James?' she said. 'You might find it interesting to see how we look after our pigs.'

Mandy's heart sank, but there was nothing for it. Neil was on his feet and already coming after them.

'So how come Five Acre doesn't have a pig unit?' Neil said, looking round as they made their way to the woods.

'Because the pigs live in arks; they're free-range,' Mandy explained.

As soon as they had closed the gate in the fence enclosing the woods, Mandy began beating a stick against the bucket. All the pigs came running through the trees.

Neil watched them, a slow grin spreading over his face. 'Hey, that's a pretty neat trick!'

Mandy and James led Neil to Copper's and Comet's pen. The pigs were waiting eagerly, their heads poking up above the metal walls. Neil's eyes widened when he saw them. 'What the heck are these?' he said. 'And what about those over there?'

'These red one are Tamworths . . .' James said, beginning to reel off the names of the different breeds.

Mandy was enjoying Neil's surprise. He seemed genuinely fascinated by all the rare breeds. She felt herself warming to him.

'Uh-oh,' she said, a few moments later. 'Those pen walls are starting to look rickety.'

James nodded. 'I'm not surprised, with those two bruisers clambering up them all the time!'

Mandy chuckled. 'You can't blame them for trying to get out.' Copper blinked at her through his sandy lashes, ears swivelling at the sound of her voice. She reached out to scratch him behind one cocked ear. 'Never mind. Just a few more days to go.'

As Neil watched, James poured some of the swill out of the bucket, and the pigs went for the food, heads down, noses and trotters in the trough. They let out little grunts of contentment, chomping everything up with their strong teeth and jaws.

Mandy looked at Neil. He seemed to have recovered from his surprise at seeing all the pigs. 'So how come this is how the pigs get their food? Can't say I think much of these low-tech, free-range methods!'

'Maybe that's because you don't know much about them,' Mandy suggested.

She was expecting a sarcastic comment, but Neil just shrugged. 'You could be right there. Go on then. Educate me.'

Mandy rose to the challenge in his voice. She tried to remember everything she had heard Pete Brady telling Daniel. She thought Neil was trying hard not to look impressed, but his blue eyes were curious under his mop of dark hair. He was watching the different pigs milling around, jostling and squealing and squabbling as they fed side by side. In the pen, Ginger and Spice were sticking their tiny snouts into the trough beside their parents.

'They all look healthy enough,' Neil said grudgingly. 'But it seems like a hit-and-miss way of looking after them. I mean – how do you know if they're getting enough vitamins and minerals?'

'I don't know,' Mandy admitted. 'With experience, I guess.'

'We've got an automatic feeding system at Nixon Manor,' Neil said proudly. 'Our pigs get a measured feed of concentrates.' He pointed across the wide expanse of field that butted up against Five Acre's woods. 'See that long grey building? That's our new pig unit. It cost Dad a packet. It's the most modern unit in the district.'

Mandy thought it looked like a giant shoe box. 'What sort of pigs have you got?'

'Landraces – hundreds of them,' Neil said. 'Good baconers they are. They fatten well and fetch a good price too. Dad looks after them really well. The new sheds are heated and ventilated. They get everything they want.' He glanced round at the jostling, grunting pigs. 'There's no way my dad would let his pigs run riot all over the place like this lot!'

'I bet they'd like to though,' Mandy whispered,

just loud enough for James to hear.

James took one look at Mandy's face. 'Er... I think the pigs have finished all the scraps. Shall we go back?'

'I've got to go, anyway,' Neil announced. 'Dad will be wondering where I am.' He turned on his heel and walked off towards the fence. Seconds later he had vaulted it. 'See you sometime!' He turned and waved, before cutting across the field and heading back towards his father's farm buildings.

Mandy and James looked at each other. 'I can't make him out,' Mandy said. 'One minute he's really interested in Five Acre's methods and then the next he's turning his nose up at them.'

James shook his head. 'Me neither.'

Mandy was in the kitchen next morning, waiting for the tasks to be given out. James, Jill and Daniel came in, just as Tom was going down the list. '... the rest of you can go along with Karen. One of our neighbours, Laura Mason, has a Jersey cow for sale and Karen's interested in buying her...'

Suddenly Karen ran into the kitchen, a panicky look on her face. 'That'll have to wait, I'm afraid!' she cried. 'There's been a leak in the dairy and there's milk everywhere!'

Five

This will take some sorting out, Mandy thought, as milk swirled around her trainers.

Tom groaned. 'What a mess! How on earth did this happen?'

'I can't understand it. A valve was open on the storage tank,' Karen said. 'I've shut it off now, but hundreds of litres of milk have been wasted. We'd better phone our customers and tell them we can't deliver any organic milk to their shops today.'

'Right,' Tom agreed. 'I'll go and do that now.' He hurried back towards the office. A few minutes later, he came into the dairy where Mandy, James and a number of volunteers were using brooms to sweep milk out into the yard.

'The shopkeepers weren't too pleased at being let down,' Tom said, shaking his head. 'And I can't say I blame them.'

'What a shame,' Mandy said, feeling sorry for Karen and Tom.

'Yes,' James agreed, as he swept vigorously.

It was late morning before the last of the milk and been swilled away with buckets of hot soapy water. Karen sat dejectedly in a kitchen chair, while Tom made tea for everyone.

'It won't look good if our sponsors get to hear of this,' Karen said. 'They won't want to donate money to a farm that's run inefficiently. Oh, dear. This couldn't have happened at a worse time.'

Tom put his arm round his wife's shoulders. 'Come on, love. Don't worry. Accidents can happen to anyone. People will understand.'

'I hope so.' Karen gave a long sigh, then stood up. 'I think I'll pop over to Laura Mason's place now. It might cheer me up. Would someone go and fetch Pete, please? He's down at Copper and Comet's pen.'

'We'll go. Won't we, James?' Mandy said at once.

Karen's face seemed to brighten at their enthusiasm. 'Any excuse to see those pigs, eh?'

They found Pete hammering a couple of nails into the corrugated iron sheeting. 'Won't be a tick,' he told them. 'I'd better just finish this. By the way, how did you get on with the Nixon lad last night?'

'OK,' James said. 'I reckon Neil's becoming interested in Five Acre.'

'Yes,' Mandy agreed. 'But it's as though he feels guilty about it or something.'

Pete squinted as he lined up a nail with a wood support. 'You might have something there, lass. His dad's always been a hard-headed practical sort. He probably fed Neil the value of profits and high yields along with his breakfast.'

'So Neil's dad wouldn't approve of him learning about organic farming?' Mandy asked.

'I should think not!' Pete said, letting out his breath on a long whistle. 'Jim Nixon makes no bones about what he thinks of Five Acre Farm. According to him, Tom and Karen are a couple of amateurs with pie-in-the-sky ideas about farming!'

What a cheek! Mandy thought. The Capthornes' methods might be different, but she was sure they were just as hard-working and practical as Neil's dad.

She thought of the tall, dark-haired boy and the way his eyes had lit up at the sight of the different breeds of pigs. He had watched them running free in the woods, a smile of genuine pleasure on his face.

'Maybe Neil's not like his dad,' she said.

Pete glanced sharply at her. 'All I'm saying is, watch out for him.' He straightened up and gave the metal wall a shake. 'Right. That should hold. Even if these two decide to give it another battering.'

Copper came trotting towards the mended wall. He reared up on his hind legs, trotters striking against the metal as he pulled himself up. Then he rested his front feet on the top of the metal sheet, his cheeky face looking up at them. Moments later, Comet's broad snout appeared and she hefted herself up beside Copper.

'They're testing that wall!' James said.

It was true, Mandy thought. She had the feeling that Copper and Comet, and their babies, weren't going to put up with being confined to their pen for too much longer.

Mandy and James sat beside Karen in the borrowed pick-up truck on the way to the smallholding. Pete and the others sat in the back.

'I've been wanting a Jersey for a while,' Karen commented. 'They give the richest milk in the world. There's nothing better for butter and cheese making.'

The smallholding was down a narrow lane, edged on both sides with dry-stone walls. Karen parked the truck in front of a grey stone house and everyone piled out.

A woman wearing a baggy hand-knitted sweater over old jeans and wellies came down the garden path to meet them. 'Hello there,' Laura Mason said, with a warm smile. 'Come on through. Marigold's in the field nearest the house.'

Marigold, the Jersey cow, turned to look at them with liquid brown eyes, her jaws working as she chewed a mouthful of grass. She had a pale fawn coat and a pretty brown face. There was a darker brown plume on the end of her tail.

'Oh,' Mandy said, the minute she saw Marigold. 'Isn't she small? She's really sweet.'

'Ah, but she has to be a good milker too. Looks aren't everything,' Pete said, in his no-nonsense way.

'True enough,' Laura said. 'That's why I'm selling her down-calving, so she's in full profit. Come and have a look at her.'

'What does down calving and in full profit mean?' James asked Karen, as Pete examined Marigold.

'It means Marigold has just calved and is giving lots of milk,' Karen told him. 'It's the best time to buy a dairy cow.'

Marigold stood chewing placidly as Pete felt her udder, looking for any hard lumps. Mandy knew he was checking for signs of mastitis.

'Is she TT?' Pete said. 'And free from brucellosis?' Laura nodded. 'She's certified free from both.

I've got the documentation in the house.'

'TT means tuberculin tested – for tuberculosis,' Mandy explained to James. 'Dad gives injections for TB early in the year. Brucellosis is another cattle disease. If a cow has either of them it's very serious and it's illegal to sell their milk.'

Having finished his examination, Pete stood up, 'She's got a bloom of health on her all right. Do you want to milk her, Karen?'

Karen nodded. 'If that's OK with you, Laura?'

'Of course. Do you want to milk her right out? Then you can judge her yield.' Laura unfastened the gate. 'I'll bring her to the cowshed.'

'Can James and I do that?' Mandy asked. She thought Marigold, with her delicate build and soft fawn coat, was one of the prettiest cows she had ever seen.

Laura smiled. 'Go ahead. Then you can see how gentle she is.'

Marigold stood there placidly, her velvety ears pointing forward, as Mandy and James approached. Mandy reached out and put her arms gently round the cow's neck and stroked her behind the ears.

'Hello there, girl,' she said softly. She tore up a handful of sweet grass and held it out. As the cow moved to nibble the grass, Mandy led her out of the field and into the cobbled farmyard. Marigold followed, her dainty hooves clopping on the cobbles.

'She's really tame, isn't she?' James said, walking alongside. He opened the cowshed door and Marigold walked inside all by herself.

Laura reached up for a bag of rolled oats. 'You can give her some of these. I usually give her a treat when I milk her.'

James tipped some oats into the manger. While Marigold was chewing them, Laura washed the cow's udder and rear end with warm water, then dried her thoroughly with a towel. 'It's important to have everything really clean before you begin milking,' she explained.

Everyone watched as Karen settled herself on a milking-stool and gripped a bucket at an angle between her knees. She took hold of the two front teats between her thumbs and forefingers. Her fingers moved in a gentle but firm rhythm as she drew down the rich, creamy milk. Mandy, James and the others watched it foaming into the bucket.

'Each teat draws milk from one quarter of the udder,' Karen explained. 'I'm checking to see that Marigold has four good quarters. Sometimes a cow will only give milk from three.'

When Karen had finished milking, she stood up and patted Marigold's fawn side. 'Good girl,' she said. She looked at Laura. 'She's a pleasure to milk.

And the milk itself looks excellent. Maybe we could all taste some?'

'Sure, come on inside the house,' Laura said. She gave them all tea, fruitcake and glasses of Marigold's milk.

'This is delicious, isn't it?' Mandy said, sipping the rich, creamy milk.

'Mmm,' James murmured, draining his glass.

'Are you going to buy Marigold, Karen?' Mandy asked.

Karen's face lit up in a smile. 'I think she'll do just fine!'

'Great!' Mandy said. 'Marigold's going to love

living at Five Acre Farm!' She was thinking of all the time she and James could spend with the little heifer.

A few minutes later the paperwork was done. Karen wrote out a cheque and handed it to Laura. 'We'll take Marigold with us,' she said. 'And I think I can count on plenty of help settling Marigold in at Five Acre!'

The little Jersey behaved beautifully on the ride back to Five Acre.

On firm ground again, Marigold looked around at the unfamiliar farmyard. Her ears swivelled and she lifted her delicate muzzle as she quested the air.

'She's bound to be nervous,' Karen said. 'We'll tie her in the cowshed and spoil her a bit until she settles down.'

In the cowshed, James tipped some barley meal into the manger. Mandy stroked the cow's soft fawn coat and rubbed her behind her velvety ears. 'You're going to love it here, Marigold,' she said.

Karen smiled. 'Right. Now let's give her time to calm down and get used to her new home. You can help me milk her tonight if you like.'

'We'd love to,' Mandy and James replied.

They left Marigold munching on the barley meal and went off to eat a late lunch in the kitchen.

After Mandy and James finished eating, Karen sent them to join Daniel, Jill and the other farm workers in the orchard. The early apple crop was ripe for picking. Wooden ladders were propped against the trees and a trailer stood ready to be loaded with brimming baskets.

'Hey! Over here, you two!' Daniel called. He was gathering up armfuls of the windfalls that lay on the ground.

Mandy and James went over to help. Some of the apples were split and bruised; their white flesh had turned brown where it had been exposed to the air.

'Ugh. Look, maggots,' James said. 'I wouldn't fancy eating windfalls.'

'No,' Mandy said. 'But I know who would – maggots and all!'

James grinned. 'Don't tell me. Copper and Comet!'

After supper, Mandy and James went on their usual jaunt down to the woods. This time, as well as the pig bucket, they had a bag of windfalls.

The setting sun cast long shadows on the mossy grass and it was cool beneath the trees. Five Acre looked peaceful, with the orchard and kitchen garden deserted and the animals grazing in the fields.

By the time Mandy and James reached the large

pen, they were surrounded by jostling, grunting bodies. There seemed even more excitement than usual in the piggy ranks. 'It's these apples,' James said. 'They're mad for them!'

'All right, all right!' Mandy laughed as she tipped food and windfalls into the outside troughs. 'Keep your bristles on!'

Copper and Comet were there too – two cheeky, sandy faces peering over the metal walls. With their curved mouths, they always looked as if they were grinning. Ginger and Spice were squealing and grunting, dashing round between their parents' legs, trying to get at the food.

'Hello, you noisy lot!' Mandy said, going straight over and making a fuss of them. She couldn't help it. Of all the animals on Five Acre, the Tamworths were her favourites. 'We've brought you a special treat tonight.'

'Yep! Wormy, bruised apples, yum, yum!' James said.

Mandy laughed. 'You'd think it was a treat if you were a pig!'

Copper and Comet scrunched up the apples straight away, apple juice and pulp dripping from their mouths. They seemed to think it was fun to bowl the apples along the ground before scooping them up.

'Look at that!' James said. 'Copper's playing football!'

Mandy chuckled. It really did look as if Copper was dribbling his apple round the pen. He was nudging it back and forth between his snout and one dainty front trotter, grunting with pleasure. Suddenly, Comet rushed him broadside. Before Copper realised what was happening, Comet had swiped the apple and run off with it. She gave a deep grunt of triumph as she chomped her prize.

'Poor old Copper. He looks really put out!' Mandy said. She dug into the box and found an apple to throw into the pen, right under Copper's nose. 'Here you are, boy. Last one!'

Copper snuffled up the apple, crunching it up double-time, glancing warily over his shoulder at Comet. But his mate was ignoring him. She was settling down to suckle her demanding babies. Copper was still ambling round the pen, his nose full of the delicious smell of apples. He looked up at Mandy and James, grunting hopefully.

'Sorry, boy,' James said. 'We haven't got any left. How about a scratch instead?' He picked up a twig and leaned into the pen.

Copper usually loved having his hide scratched, but he seemed distracted tonight. He kept rooting about, pushing his nose into the churned-up soil as if trying to get the very last little scrap of delicious apple.

'Copper really loved those windfalls, didn't he?' Mandy said, as she and James strolled back to the farmhouse.

As they walked across the yard, Mandy saw a tall figure leaning against the farm gate. It was Neil Nixon. 'Hi, you two,' he said, strolling towards them. 'I was waiting for you. Are you going inside?'

Mandy and James nodded.

'I'll come in with you then,' Neil decided boldly.

'Er . . .' James said, looking across at Mandy.

Across the yard, Karen popped her head round the door of the cowshed. 'Oh, you've got Neil with you,' she called out, looking surprised. 'I'm just about to milk Marigold. Do you want to come and watch, Neil?'

'Yeah, right. Thanks,' Neil spoke up eagerly.

Inside the cowshed, Mandy breathed in the sweet, clean smell. Marigold was nibbling oats from the manger. She turned her head and looked at them with placid dark eyes. 'She seems to have settled in already,' James said.

Karen washed and dried Marigold's udder, then asked Mandy if she wanted to have a go at milking.

'Yes, please.' Mandy settled herself on the stool.

'Put your fingers where I showed you earlier,'

Karen said. 'That's right. Good. Squeeze the top of the teat gently to stop the milk going back up. Now – you have to squeeze downwards, one finger at a time, in quick succession.'

'I've never seen anyone milking by hand,' Neil said, watching closely. 'It looks a bit like rubbing your tummy and tapping your head at the same time!'

Karen chuckled. 'It is rather like that.'

Mandy felt self-conscious with Neil watching, but she followed Karen's instructions. To her surprise, the milk began to flow into the bucket. It was very slow, nothing like when Karen was milking, but she was pleased with her success. 'Good girl, Marigold,' she said softly.

After a few minutes, she stood up and took the bucket over to the metal churn that stood in a corner. Karen showed her how to filter the milk through a strainer, then close the churn lid.

'Do you want to have a go?' Karen asked Neil.

He shook his head vigorously. 'No way! I'll stick to milking machines, thanks!'

'All right.' Karen smiled. 'How about you, James?'

James blushed and threw Mandy a panicky look. But Mandy reminded him of the time he had milked their friend Lydia's goat up at High Cross Farm. 'You were really good at it,' she said.

James grinned. 'I was, wasn't I? OK then.' He sat down and began to milk. Marigold never stirred until James had finished. She just chewed on the rolled oats and took no notice as the milk frothed into the bucket.

Then Karen took over, and the churn was soon full. After they had settled Marigold down for the night, they all went towards the dairy. Karen began pouring some of the milk into a cream separator.

'Do you mind if I use your bathroom, Karen?' Neil asked politely.

'You go ahead,' said Karen. 'Do you remember where it is, from the other day?'

Neil nodded and went off to the farmhouse. Mandy and James waited behind with Karen, until she had finished in the dairy.

'I think I'll go and phone Mum and Dad, if that's all right, Karen,' Mandy said, when they were back in the farmhouse.

'Course it is, love,' Karen said. 'Why don't you use the phone in my office?'

'Say hello from me,' James called out, as Mandy went into the hall and closed the kitchen door behind her.

Suddenly the office door opened and Neil came out. He looked shocked when he saw Mandy. 'Er . . . I got lost,' he said quickly, looking flustered. 'I thought that was the door into the kitchen.' In a panicky rush, he barged past Mandy, almost knocking her over, and loped towards the front door. A moment later, it slammed behind him.

Mandy blinked. Neil Nixon was one weird boy. He hadn't even bothered to say goodbye. Inside Karen's office, she picked up the phone and dialled home. It gave her a good feeling to imagine the phone ringing in the stone cottage.

Mrs Hope answered the phone. 'Hello, Animal Ark.'

'Hi, Mum,' Mandy said. 'It's me. How's everything there?'

'Hello, love!' Mrs Hope said. 'Oh, you know, the usual stuff. Sick budgies, kittens with sore paws, dogs who've eaten something to upset them. Your dad's just popped out to the Animal Sanctuary. Betty Hilder's had an injured squirrel brought in.'

'Oh,' Mandy said, immediately concerned. 'What's wrong with it?'

'It was hit by a car, but it was only a glancing blow – it had a lucky escape,' her mum said reassuringly. 'How are you and James getting on?'

'Great,' Mandy said. 'James said to say hello. It's brilliant here. The best holiday ever!'

'Hmm. And would that be because you're spending most of the time with animals?'

Mandy laughed. 'I suppose it is!'

A few minutes later she said goodbye. 'Give my love to Dad. I'll phone again in a few days.'

As she went back down the hall, she heard the sound of Tom's guitar in the kitchen. 'Uh-oh,' she groaned. It looked as if everyone was in for another of his sing-songs!

Six

Some days later, James, Mandy and some other helpers headed for a stretch of dry-stone wall that lined the road between Five Acre and Nixon Manor. Some of the stones had toppled, leaving gaps in the wall.

Pete was busy using his expert judgement to sort the stone into sizes. He was wearing his usual working uniform of dark-blue overalls and a cloth cap jammed down low on his forehead.

'I wonder if Pete ever takes his cap off!' James joked.

'Don't!' Mandy had to stifle a giggle as she imagined him wearing it sitting in the bath!

For a while the helpers worked alongside Pete.

Mandy reckoned that building up the stretch of wall was a bit like doing a three-dimensional jigsaw puzzle. She looked up from putting a stone in place and saw that there was a tractor at work on Nixon Manor Farm.

'That's Neil driving, isn't it?' James said, shading his eyes with his hand.

'I think so.' Mandy craned her neck as the tractor chugged past. 'He hasn't been over since the night he watched us milk Marigold, has he?'

'No,' James agreed. 'I wonder why not.'

'It was funny, the way he rushed out of the front door like that,' Mandy said.

'Is that what he did? Maybe he had to get back home, before his dad got suspicious,' Pete suggested, wiping his hands on a handkerchief that had seen better days. 'Neil looks up to his dad. He wouldn't want to get into his bad books.'

'But he really seems to like spending time at Five Acre,' Mandy said.

'Aye, lass,' Pete said. 'But he wouldn't want to risk his dad's anger and disapproval. Course, he could have other reasons for hanging around here . . .' he hinted darkly.

'What reasons?' James wanted to know.

But all Pete would say was, 'I've got my suspicions. And I'm keeping them to myself.'

Mandy looked at James and raised her eyebrows. None of it made any sense to her.

Half an hour later, the repairs to the wall were finished. The new stretch of walling blended in well. Mandy wondered if their bit would last for hundreds of years. She felt pleased to have contributed to something that would be around for so long.

Mandy and James joined the other helpers for lunch. For once, Karen didn't put in an appearance.

'I wonder where Karen is,' James said. 'Come to think of it, I haven't seen her for ages.'

'She must be here,' Mandy said. 'The Land-rover's in the drive.'

Tom seemed quiet during the meal, and when the lunch things had been cleared away he allocated the jobs for the afternoon. 'Mandy and James, you're with Daniel and Jill on pigs . . .'

Jill tutted. 'Oh, well. I suppose I might as well get a look at these precious pigs,' she said grumpily, stomping off into the yard.

Mandy and James hung back in the kitchen – suspicious that something was amiss and anxious to ask Tom if they could help in any way.

'Are you two still here?' Tom joked, a few minutes later, when everyone else had gone to do their jobs.

'We thought something might be wrong,' Mandy

said. 'And wondered if there was anything we could do, didn't we, James?'

James nodded.

'Thanks,' Tom said. 'But I don't think you can. We've had some worrying news. Some of our biggest sponsors are having doubts about renewing their sponsorship. Karen's been on the phone for hours, trying to persuade them to keep up their donations.'

'But why have they changed their minds?' Mandy said.

Tom's face was grim. 'Who knows? Karen thinks Jim Nixon's behind this. She could be right.'

'But Five Acre's brilliant!' Mandy fumed.

'Yeah!' James said indignantly. 'Anyone would have to be mad to listen to him!'

'Thanks for the vote of confidence,' Tom said, 'But I'm sure you've heard the phrase "mud sticks". Anyway, you two go on down and help Pete with the pigs. Daniel and Jill are probably down there by now.'

'OK,' Mandy and James replied.

'This is just awful,' Mandy said. 'Remember that brochure we were reading in the car, on the way here?'

James nodded. 'Yes. What about it?'

'It said that all the farms owned by the Trust rely heavily on sponsorship. Five Acre could be in big trouble.'

* * *

Mandy and James had just entered the woods when Daniel and Jill came running towards them.

'Now what?' Mandy groaned.

'We can't find Copper and Comet,' Daniel panted.

'Or the piglets!' Jill said.

Mandy was already dashing through the trees, James at her heels. As they drew close to the pen, there was an unnerving silence.

'Maybe they haven't checked the pig house,' James suggested hopefully.

Mandy moved round the outside wall, an inkling of what had happened forming in her mind. She saw the wooden post all askew, and a sheet of corrugated iron bent up at the corner. There were a few ginger colored hairs attached to the edge of the metal sheet.

'They've escaped,' she announced. 'We've *got* to find them!'

'Er . . . I think we already have. Look!' James pointed through the trees.

Two large reddish shapes and two small pink blobs were making their way along the edge of Jim Nixon's wheatfield.

Mandy's eyes widened in horror. 'Oh, heck,' she moaned. 'We're going to need help. If they get into that cornfield they'll be in big trouble!'

'Don't you mean pig trouble?' Daniel quipped.

Mandy was in no mood for jokes. She headed back
to the farmhouse, James, Jill and Daniel in tow. Her
mind was working overtime, trying to fasten on to
an idea. Suddenly she had it.

She shot across the farmyard and straight into
the kitchen. 'Quick! Pig bucket!' she gasped. 'And I
need apples!'

Karen was at the sink. She turned and blinked at
Mandy. 'If you're that hungry I can make you a
sandwich,' she joked.

Mandy blurted out the story of the pigs' escape
and her idea for luring them back to their pen.

'Right!' Karen became all action. Grabbing the
bucket from under the sink, she emptied a basket
of apples into it, then thrust it at Mandy. 'I'll find
Tom and Pete and get them to meet you in Nixon's
wheatfield.'

Mandy and James raced back towards the woods
and shinned over the fence. They could see
Copper, Comet, Ginger and Spice, strolling along,
munching at the wheat at the edge of the field.

'They haven't gone *into* the corn yet!' James
gasped.

'Look!' Mandy pointed to Jim and Neil, who were
running down the side of the field. Coming towards
the Nixons, from the opposite direction, were the
Capthornes.

'Uh-oh! Now what?' James asked.

If everyone starts shouting, it'll panic the pigs, Mandy thought quickly. Copper and Comet had raised their heads. One false move and they'd take off. She remembered why Comet was called Comet. If it came to a chase, they'd never catch the pigs.

'Just copy me!' she hissed to James. 'OK?'

He didn't argue, but his eyebrows rose as Mandy picked up a stick and banged it against the bucket. She walked boldly towards the pigs, praying that she'd reach them before Jim Nixon or one of his men got there and ruined her plan.

Mandy saw Copper take a step towards her. Then Comet followed her mate's lead. 'It's working,' she whispered to James.

The windfalls rolled about in the metal bucket, releasing delightful fruity odours. Copper and Comet edged closer, snouts lifted, snuffling at the air, Ginger and Spice trotted along at their parents' heels. Mandy picked out a juicy apple and threw it towards Copper.

James jumped in astonishment as a few hundred kilograms of muscular Tamworth put on a sudden spurt. Oinking happily, Copper and Comet hurtled down the side of the field towards Mandy, dainty trotters barely touching the grass.

'Cripes!' James gasped. 'Now what?'

'We lead them back to the pigpen,' Mandy said,
setting off at a run towards the fence.

Almost there. Just a few more metres, Mandy thought. It
was a good thing, because she was nearly out of
apples and she had a stitch.

'Here you are,' she said, pausing to throw another
windfall to Comet. One gobble and it was gone.
Comet gave a warning squeal to a huge Gloucester
Old Spot who dared to try to steal an apple from
Ginger and Spice. Copper was squabbling with a
Berkshire, shouldering the smaller pig aside.

'Here they come!' James called out to Pete, who

had quickly summed up the situation and managed to hurry back to the pen.

'Oh, my!' Pete spluttered with laughter. 'Now I've seen it all!'

Mandy and James marched towards the pigpen followed by Copper, Comet, Ginger, Spice – and every other pig on Five Acre! She hadn't had time to think her brilliant plan through and it had worked rather too well.

With Pete's help, Copper and Comet and their family were finally lured back into their pen. They snuffled round, rooting at the last few apples, taking no notice as Pete repaired the wall. The other pigs hung around outside for a while, then, losing interest as the food ran out, wandered back through the trees.

'That was some quick thinking, lass,' Pete Brady said.

Mandy beamed, pleased that her plan had worked. Then her smile faded as she saw Karen and Tom approaching. Behind them was Jim Nixon, his face like thunder.

'Those pigs could have done untold damage to my wheat!' The bullying voice reached Mandy and James.

'But thanks to Mandy and James they didn't, did they?' Karen said sweetly.

Jim Nixon was still red-faced and blustering. 'Can't even control their animals . . .' he muttered. 'What did I tell you, Neil? Call themselves farmers!'

'Yeah, right.' Neil hung his head, looking embarrassed.

Mandy felt sorry for him. The boy seemed to want to remain loyal to his father, but she could see that he hated being in the middle of this disagreement.

Tom looked about to speak, but Karen put her hand on his arm. 'I'll handle this,' she whispered, just loud enough for Mandy to hear. 'Jim,' she said, more loudly. 'I'm sorry for putting you to any trouble. I accept full responsibility and I will, of course, pay for any damage.'

Jim Nixon's mouth dropped open. 'Well – there's no damage, as such . . .'

'Maybe not,' Karen went on, 'but it's the inconvenience, isn't it? You've had to dash all the way over here. The least I can do is offer you a cup of tea and a slice of my home-made fruitcake.'

'No need for that . . .' Nixon muttered, starting to turn away. 'Come on, Neil . . .'

'Oh, but I insist,' Karen said, swooping forward with a winning smile. She began ushering the still-protesting farmer towards the farmhouse.

Tom winked at Mandy and James. 'He doesn't

stand a chance! Not when Karen's in that mood!'

Mandy could almost feel sorry for Jim Nixon, as he perched on the edge of one of the comfy kitchen chairs. *It must be torture for him, having to be so polite,* she thought.

He listened to Karen's description of her plans for the fund-raising. He listened to her idea about extending the farm shop. But when she began explaining how complicated it was to be a manager for a charitable trust and how very difficult it was to have to rely on sponsorship, he jumped up, a panicky look in his eye.

'Well, it's been very pleasant,' the farmer murmured. 'We'd better be going now . . .'

'Must you?' Karen crooned. 'Well – only if you and Neil agree to come to our fund-raising picnic. Remember – we're having a brass band and a marquee . . .'

'Er . . . I don't know . . .' Nixon began.

Mandy hid a smile, as Karen brushed away his uncertainty with a wave of her hand. 'Oh, I absolutely insist.'

'All right. All right, We'll come,' Nixon said desperately. 'Neil! We're leaving – right now!'

Neil didn't need telling twice. He leaped to his feet and marched to the door. No one had mentioned his visits to Five Acre. Mandy thought Neil looked as if he couldn't believe his lucky escape.

After the Nixons left, Tom erupted into delighted laughter. 'I can't believe it,' he cried, kissing Karen on the cheek. 'You've got Jim to agree to come to our fund-raising. He won't back down now, his pride won't let him!'

Karen's smile wavered. 'All I've got to do now is persuade our sponsors to give generously,' she said. 'And that could be a lot more difficult.'

Seven

Several nights later, Mandy was trying not to think about Five Acre Farm's money worries as she joined James, Daniel and Pete on pig patrol. It was too awful to imagine what might happen to the animals if Karen failed to get enough sponsorship.

The picnic and farm open day just has to be brilliant, she thought. Then loads of people would want to donate money.

She helped James tip pig food into the troughs, while Daniel and Pete changed the drinking water. Then the stockman went off to do his evening rounds. 'You three can stay here now, if you like,' he said over his shoulder. 'I can manage.'

'OK!' Mandy, James and Daniel didn't argue.

Mandy looked up and saw Neil coming through the woods. 'Look who's coming,' she said, digging James in the ribs.

'Hi!' Neil came up to them with a wide grin. 'That was a pretty neat trick with the pigs the other day.'

'Thanks,' Mandy and James said.

'I never knew you could get pigs to behave like that,' Neil said.

'Well – these are special pigs!' she said.

'Pete says it's because they haven't had the character bred out of them,' Daniel chipped in.

'They're more intelligent than dogs,' James confirmed.

All this praise seemed too much for Neil. 'Hang on! They ran away in the first place!'

Mandy nodded. 'But I reckon Copper and Comet knew just what they were doing. They ended up getting another treat of apples, didn't they? Comet runs at the speed of light. If she'd really wanted to leg it, we'd never have caught her!'

'You'll be telling me those two can do crossword puzzles next!'

Mandy laughed. She didn't mind Neil's teasing. She was convinced that Copper and Comet were smarter than the average pig.

'They're gorgeous though, aren't they? Especially the babies,' Daniel said, looking admiringly at

Ginger and Spice, who were jostling for their share of food. 'I'm going to ask my parents if I can have some pet pigs when I go home.'

Mandy gave a horrified gasp. 'But you live in the middle of a town! Pigs need lots of land. You can't keep them in a small garden.'

'Who said I had a small garden?' Daniel challenged. 'And I know what pigs need! I've been looking after these for well over a week!'

Mandy hoped that Daniel didn't really mean it. She knew what happened to pets that outgrew their homes. Welford Animal Sanctuary was full of them.

Neil was watching the mass of grunting pigs outside the pen. 'You know,' he said, 'I reckon it's a shame you don't get to see these old breeds much.'

Mandy gave him a sharp look to see if he was serious. She decided he was. 'My dad says most pig farmers prefer modern hybrids that fatten quickly,' she said.

'I can't argue with that,' Neil said. 'You'd have to look at different ways of farming if you wanted to keep traditional breeds. And I can just see my dad giving *that* idea headroom!'

After they had finished their food, the pigs ambled up to the fence, grunting loudly, bristly red noses snuffling the air. Despite his muscular bulk,

Copper gave a dainty backward skip and oinked loudly.

'He's asking to be scratched,' Mandy said. 'Pigs love that.' She picked up a twig and gave it to Neil. 'Here you are. Why don't you have a go?'

Neil hesitated, looking embarrassed. 'Don't be daft!'

'Haven't you ever scratched a pig with a twig before?' James asked in his usual straightforward way.

'Nah!' Neil gave a narrow grin and shook his head. 'We don't go in for making a silly fuss of animals on our farm. Pigs mean profit to my dad, and that's all.'

'But it's not making a silly fuss,' Mandy retorted. 'It's keeping them happy. Surely your dad hasn't got anything against that?'

'My dad's all right,' Neil said defensively. 'You just don't know him.'

'No,' Mandy admitted, thinking it was best not to get on to this subject. She waggled the stick encouragingly. 'Go on, Neil, try it. You might like it!'

Neil kicked at a tuft of grass. Then he shrugged. 'Oh, give it here then!' he said, snatching the twig out of her hand.

Reaching out, he touched Comet's back with the

tip of the twig. She let out a soft grunt and started jiggling about, pushing against the stick. Neil started grinning. He scratched harder and Comet grunted with delight, flexing her shoulder and lifting her chin.

'See? She loves it,' Mandy said. 'She's showing you where else to scratch her.'

'Yeah. She is, isn't she?' A grin spread across Neil's face as he scratched Comet under the chin. 'You know, it sounds daft, but I've never really bothered much with getting to know pigs. They've always just been there.' Neil gazed admiringly at Comet, who was now going into raptures as he scratched her behind one ear.

Mandy and James exchanged a pleased look. Neil seemed a different person when he was around pigs!

'I reckon Neil ought to start camping out on Five Acre,' James joked, as he, Mandy and a few other helpers helped Tom sweep out the empty barn.

'I know!' Mandy said with a grin. 'He's been over here nearly every night this week. I'm not sure if it's us he comes to see or Copper and Comet.'

Tom leaned on his broom. 'He was quizzing me about whether our pigs ever get pneumonia last night in the kitchen. I even caught him sneaking a look at my organic farming magazine. You know,

Karen's convinced Neil's got a good head on his shoulders. Maybe he's starting to think for himself.'

He set to with the broom again, causing a cloud of dust to fly up. 'Come on, you lot. We'd better finish clearing out this barn. Karen wants to show it to the sponsors on Sunday. If we don't get it spick and span, she'll have my guts for garters!'

On their return to the farmhouse, they found Karen sitting at her office desk. Papers and notes littered the desk top and a cold cup of coffee stood at one side.

Tom took one look at the mess. 'I'm going to make a fresh pot of tea. Would you like one?'

Karen gave a weary smile and let out a long sigh. 'Thanks, you're a life-saver. You wouldn't think that an open day, a picnic and a musical event would be such hard work to organise. Oh, bother . . . ' she said, as a pile of papers slid sideways and dropped to the floor.

'I'll get them.' Mandy began to gather them up.

'Shall I make the tea?' James asked tactfully.

'Thanks, lad,' Tom said. 'We'll join you in the kitchen in a few minutes.' He patted his wife's shoulder. 'I'm sure everything will turn out all right, love.'

Karen's smile was strained. 'I expect it will. It's just that this event is so important for us. We really

need those donations and pledges. I'm doing all I can to encourage people to be generous.'

'I'll say you are!' Tom raised one sandy eyebrow. 'A brass band, a marquee with a dance floor, and a posh spread. And I know just what that'll be like. Posh bits and pieces on sticks and sandwiches you can eat in one bite.'

Mandy chuckled.

'We're not feeding a bunch of farm workers, you know. These are business men, pen-pushers mostly – and their glamorous wives!' Karen said, riffling through the papers Mandy had handed back to her. 'Where's my list? I need to find that before I can stop for a break.'

Tom bent to kiss her cheek. 'OK. But tea straight afterwards. Farmer's orders!'

Half an hour later, Karen was looking more relaxed. 'Ah, that's better. There's nothing like a cup of tea to perk you up,' she said, pouring herself another cup. 'I'll milk Marigold when I've finished this one. Anyone fancy bringing her in from the field for me?'

'Need you ask?' Tom said with a grin, as Mandy and James both jumped up.

The sun was setting as they walked across the field to Marigold. Layers of cloud were piled overhead, the edges glowing silver and gold.

'Come on, girl,' Mandy said, stroking Marigold's fawn ears. 'Time for you to go to the milking shed.'

Usually a few soft words were all Marigold needed to begin following them. But today she blew through her nostrils and moved sideways.

'That's funny,' James said. 'Why's she doing that?'

'I don't know.' Mandy looking closely at the little Jersey cow. 'She looks OK.' After some determined coaxing, Marigold came out of her field readily enough. But Mandy, knowing that animals could be sick before the symptoms showed up clearly, decided it was best not to take any chances.

Once in the cowshed, she mentioned Marigold's restlessness to Karen.

'There's nothing outwardly wrong with her,' Karen said, after giving Marigold a careful check over. She settled down on to her milking-stool, then squirted a little milk into her hand.

'Why are you doing that?' Mandy asked.

'I'm checking for clots. Mastitis is the obvious thing to look for. In the early stages there are no outward signs but there are clots in the milk.'

Mandy looked at the milk. It was smooth and creamy.

'Milk's fine,' Karen said. 'No sign of mastitis there.' She patted Marigold's side. 'She's probably just having an off day. We're all allowed one of those occasionally! I'll get Pete to check her later.'

Marigold stood quietly during the milking, but was once again restless when Mandy and James led her back to the field. At one point she began making lowing noises of complaint. Mandy frowned. This just wasn't like the normally placid Marigold. She couldn't get rid of the feeling that something was wrong.

Mandy decided to phone home again before going up to bed.

Mr Hope answered on the second ring.

'That was quick,' Mandy said. 'Hi, Dad!'

'Hello, Mandy love,' Mr Hope said. 'I've just got back from treating a sheep with an eye inflammation and – before you ask – it's going to be fine! Anyway, how about you? Are you missing home?'

'A bit,' Mandy admitted. 'But not much!'

'It's nice to know you're wanted,' Mr Hope said, mournfully.

'Oh, Dad!' Mandy grinned. 'You know what I mean. Besides, it's only a few days until you come and see me. You and Mum are still taking a long weekend, aren't you?'

'Wild horses wouldn't stop me,' Mr Hope said.

'We're booked in at Tor View guesthouse from tomorrow. I can already smell that air up on the high moors. Your mum and I intend to start out early and get down to some serious hillwalking. Ah, here's your mum now. She wants a word, so I'll say goodbye. See you soon, love.'

A few minutes later, Mandy said goodbye to her mum and put down the phone.

The following morning, Mandy woke early and couldn't get back to sleep. At the back of her mind there was that niggling worry about Marigold.

She dressed quickly so as not to disturb Jill, then slipped quietly out of the room. Karen was already up and in the kitchen, preparing breakfast for everyone to eat later.

'Hello, Mandy,' Karen said. 'First up today? I couldn't sleep either for thinking about this fundraising. It's only two days away now.'

'Shall I bring Marigold in for milking for you?' Mandy offered.

'Would you? Thanks, love. I'll just finish up here, then I'll come out.'

Mandy strode out, hardly noticing the brightness of the morning. She'd be able to relax once she'd checked Marigold was fine. But as she approached the field, she saw the Jersey cow standing by the hedge, her head drooping down.

All Mandy's worries rushed to the surface. She pulled open the gate and dashed across the field. When she got close to Marigold, she could see that the cow looked lopsided. Her left-hand side was swollen, big and tight, like a drum. Marigold was lowing mournfully, obviously in pain.

'Oh, you poor thing,' Mandy gasped. 'Stay there, Marigold. I'll get help!'

She turned on her heel and broke into a run.

Eight

Mandy ran as fast as she could across the farmyard and into the kitchen.

'Karen!' she called. 'Something's wrong with Marigold! Come quickly!'

'I'm on my way.' Karen followed her quickly across the yard.

'What's the matter with her?' Mandy asked.

'It looks like bloat,' Karen said. 'It's something ruminants get. If the normal rumen gases don't get released, an animal can blow up like a balloon.'

Mandy knew that ruminants were animals like cows, sheep and goats. They had extra stomachs called rumens, for digesting grass.

'I'll have to run back to the house and phone the

vet,' Karen said. 'Will you be all right staying here with Marigold?'

Mandy nodded. 'I'm used to sick animals.'

Karen flashed her a grateful smile. 'Good girl. I'll be back as soon as I can.'

Mandy spoke softly to Marigold, knowing that reassuring sick animals helped to lower their blood pressure. 'Help's on its way,' she soothed. 'Don't worry. You're going to be fine.'

But the poor animal kept turning her head and trying to bite her painfully swollen side. The next few minutes felt like hours to Mandy. At last she saw Karen hurrying towards her. 'The vet's been called out on another emergency,' the farm manager told her. 'He won't be back for hours. Tom's phoned Pete Brady. He's on his way.'

'Will he know what to do?' Mandy asked worriedly. She knew that bloat was an emergency.

Karen nodded. 'He's bound to know a country remedy, but I'd feel happier if a vet could take a look at Marigold as well.'

Mandy bit her lip. If only her mum and dad were nearer. Then she remembered something her dad had said. 'Mum and Dad might already be in Holtwick,' she said eagerly. 'They were going to be arriving especially early to go hillwalking.'

Just then Tom arrived. He had heard her mention

her parents. 'In that case, it's possible they'd have dropped off their luggage,' he said. 'Do you know which guesthouse they're staying at?'

'Yes. Tor View.'

'Right, I know the place. They stay open round the clock, as walkers turn up at all hours. I'll phone them right away.' Tom hurried away across the field.

Poor Marigold was lowing with pain and her eyes were half closed. Mandy felt helpless in the face of the little Jersey's suffering. She hoped like mad that Tom would be able to contact her parents.

Tom had only just gone back to the farmhouse, when a familiar figure in dark-blue overalls and cap came running across the field.

'Oh, thank goodness,' Karen said.

Pete arrived out of breath and red in the face. He was carrying a box of bicarbonate of soda and a length of tubing. He took in the situation at a glance.

'It's bloat all right,' he said to Karen. 'I've seen it before. We have to keep Marigold moving, but gently does it. We don't want to cause her undue stress.'

'Come on, girl. Easy now.' Karen urged the cow to take a few steps. 'Tom's trying to get a message to Mandy's parents. What can we do in the meantime, Pete?'

Pete was unrolling the tubing. 'Bicarbonate of soda often works. We'll need to dissolve 100 grams in warm water. Then dilute that down and give it as a drench.'

'I'm not sure . . .' Karen frowned, as Marigold's lowing increased. 'Do you feel confident about putting in a stomach tube?'

'I've not done it in a while,' Pete said uncertainly. 'But if there's nothing else for it . . .'

Mandy could see Karen agonising over making a decision.

'OK.' Karen nodded shortly. 'Best go and make up the drench.'

Oh, please be within reach, Mum and Dad, Mandy said silently to herself. She had seen her parents give drenches and knew there was a risk of drowning an animal by pouring liquid into its lungs by mistake.

Pete soon returned with a brimming bucket and the tubing. Mandy held her breath, as Pete carefully fed the tube into the cow's stomach. His normally ruddy face was pale and he looked nervous.

'I'm just not sure if that tube's placed right,' he said to Karen.

'There's a way of checking,' Mandy spoke up. 'Dad always puts his head against an animal's side.'

'Why's he do that?' Pete asked.

'He listens for stomach noises,' Mandy said. 'When he hears them, he knows he hasn't put the tube into the lungs by mistake.'

'It's worth a try.' Pete leaned forward and placed his ear against Marigold's side, then gave a gap-toothed grin. 'Mandy's right! I can hear stomach noises.'

Pete seemed more confident now, Mandy thought. But *her* stomach was still tight with nerves; she wished her mum or dad were here to supervise.

Suddenly there was the sound of a car arriving. Mandy looked up and saw her parents' four-wheel drive. She almost went weak with relief.

Moments later, Emily Hope was opening the gate and coming towards her, red hair glowing in the early morning sun. She wore a fleece top and walking boots.

Mandy flew across the field towards her parents and gave them each a huge hug. 'Mum! Dad! Am I glad to see you!' she breathed.

'Hello, Mandy, love,' Emily Hope said. 'We were just about to make our way up to the moors. Luckily Dad left his mobile phone number at the guesthouse. We got Tom's message and came straight over.'

Mandy flashed them a quick grin. 'Quick, Dad, over here! Marigold's really sick. Pete was about to give her a drench.'

He nodded. 'For bloat. Yes, love. Tom filled me in on the phone.'

Pete stood up as they reached him. He looked relieved. 'I'm more than happy to let the two experts take over.'

Mrs Hope stood with her arm round Mandy, while Mr Hope examined Marigold.

'You're right. It is bloat,' he said after a few minutes. 'And bicarbonate of sodium's an old remedy that often does the trick.' He looked at Pete. 'This tube's well placed.'

'Thanks to Mandy showing us a trick or two,' Karen put in.

Mr Hope smiled. 'That's my girl. OK, Pete, do you want to steady Marigold while I give the drench?'

Pete squared his shoulders. 'Right you are.'

Mrs Hope oversaw the process, while Pete kept Marigold calm. Then Mr Hope removed the stomach tube. A few minutes later there were gurgling noises from the cow's insides as she began releasing trapped gases.

'It's working!' Mandy exclaimed.

Karen stroked Marigold's fawn coat. 'Clever girl. Let it all out.'

'You can see her side starting to go down,' Mandy said. 'I bet she's beginning to feel better now!'

Mr Hope opened the emergency bag, which was always kept in the car. 'I'll just give Marigold an injection for the stress . . . There. She ought to be as right as rain in a few hours. But one of us can pop over and have a look at her tomorrow, if you like.'

Mrs Hope nodded. 'Seeing as we'll be in the area for the weekend!'

Karen smiled gratefully. 'Oh, dear. I thought this was supposed to be your weekend break!'

Mrs Hope's green eyes were warm. 'Don't worry. We're used to this. It's one of the hazards of our profession!'

Mandy went over to Marigold. She put her arms round the cow's neck and gently stroked her soft ears. 'It's all worth it, though, isn't it? To see Marigold looking better?'

'Come on back to the farmhouse, everyone,' Karen said with a grin. 'The least I can do is offer you breakfast.'

As they walked into the farmyard, a bedroom window opened and James's dark tousled head appeared. 'Hey! What's all the noise?' he called, blinking sleepily behind his glasses. 'Oh hi there, Mr and Mrs Hope!'

Mandy grinned up at James. 'You've missed all the excitement. Come on down and we'll tell you about it!'

* * *

After breakfast, Mandy and James took Mr and Mrs Hope down to the woods to see Copper, Comet, Ginger and Spice, who were now out of quarantine and enjoying rooting around in the woods with the other pigs.

Pete Brady met them at the gate, toolbox in hand.

'What's going on?' Mandy said.

Pete grinned mysteriously. 'Stand over there a minute and you'll see for yourself.'

A muscular red shape headed towards them, dainty trotters skimming over the grass.

'Copper!' Mandy said. She might have guessed!

The huge pig trundled straight up to the gate. Daintily, he thrust his nose under the catch. He gave a satisfied little grunt, and jerked his chin upwards. The metal catch held, but only just. Mandy could see that with a bit more brute force the gate would be open and Copper would be off on his explorations again – his family in tow!

'The cheeky thing,' she said with a chuckle.

'What are you going to do about the gate, Pete?' James asked.

'Fit a pig-proof wire loop, that's what!' Pete told him.

'I hope it's Copper-proof!' Mandy joked.

'I wonder how he worked out how to unlatch it?'

James exclaimed, pushing his floppy fringe off his face.

'I told you Tamworths were smart,' Pete said, sorting out his tools.

'This one's certainly a real character,' Mr Hope agreed.

'How's your handwriting?' Karen said to Mandy and James, later that same afternoon.

'It's fairly neat,' Mandy said.

'How about you, James?'

'It's readable!' James said. 'But it's not always tidy.'

Karen smiled. 'That's good enough. You haven't got to write an essay! I just need someone to write out some last-minute invitations.'

Mandy and James went with Karen to her office, where she cleared a space for them on her desk.

'I sent the official invitations to our larger sponsors weeks ago,' she explained, giving them a pile of printed, gold-embossed cards. 'But having some of them expressing doubts over the last couple of days has got me worried.'

'So – who are these for?' James asked.

'Small businesses in Holtwick who were on my list of possibles,' Karen said, giving them a list. 'I'm ready to invite anyone at this point!'

Mandy and James began writing names in the

spaces left on the printed invitations. Mandy had a sudden thought. 'Did you find the list you lost, Karen?'

The farm manager shook her head. 'It's a mystery to me where it went.'

'Was it important?' James asked.

'Oh, yes,' Karen replied. 'It was my complete schedule for the fund-raising. The caterers' menu, times of arrival, marquee hire, and details about the York Top Brass – that's the band I've hired for Sunday. Luckily, I had most of the information stored on computer.'

Half an hour later, Mandy put the last invitation

into its envelope and sealed the flap. She put the envelope on the pile with the others. 'Finished!' she said.

'Me too,' James said.

Karen looked up from entering figures in a ledger. She smiled. 'You two have been a real help. These farm accounts are taking me ages. I'd have been up until midnight if I'd had to do those invitations as well. Would you take them straight over to Tom, please? He's going to post them when he finishes at the paddock.'

'OK.' Mandy and James made for the door.

They found Tom in Hazel's paddock, with Daniel, Jill and some of the other helpers. Neil Nixon was there too. Mandy saw with surprise that Neil was holding up one of the horse's feet, so that Tom could check it over. The older boy had his back towards Hazel's flank. He was supporting the heavy leg joint with cupped hands.

'You sure you've never done this before, lad?' Tom asked him.

'Never,' Neil said. 'I'm a dab hand with tractors and combine harvesters, but I've never had the chance to work with horses.'

'Pity,' Tom remarked. 'You've got a natural gift for it. Hazel wouldn't be standing still like this if she didn't trust you.'

Neil flushed, but he looked pleased.

Mandy held up the wadge of invitations, which was secured with a rubber band. 'Karen said to give you these last-minute invitations to post, Tom,' she said.

'Oh, right.' Tom looked up. 'Put them in my jacket pocket, would you? It's hanging on the fence.'

Mandy did as he asked, tucking the envelopes securely in the inside pocket. They were a tight fit, but they all went in. Neil glanced across at her, then went back to concentrating on helping Tom.

Half an hour later, Tom stood up. 'Thanks, Neil,' he said. 'You've done a good job.'

Neil patted Hazel's muscular shoulder. 'Good girl,' he said gently. 'Well – I'd best be getting back home, Tom. See you later, everyone.'

Mandy and James and the others waved as Neil went across the paddock. Mandy saw Neil pause and lean on the fence.

A moment later she joined the others in making a fuss of Hazel. Tom had brought a packet of peppermints. Hazel crunched up the treat with her strong yellow teeth.

'She loves those, doesn't she?' Mandy said, stroking the horse's soft muzzle. She looked up to see Neil striding out across the farmyard and heading for the gate. He seemed to be in a hurry.

'OK, everyone,' Tom said, slinging his jacket over his shoulder. 'Time for a tea break.'

Tom paused outside the farmhouse. 'I'd best pop into Holtwick to the post office,' he said. 'Otherwise these invitations won't get there.' He reached inside his jacket. 'That's funny. They're not there.'

'I definitely put them in there,' Mandy said.

'Maybe you dropped them in the paddock, Tom,' James suggested.

'It's possible,' Tom agreed, 'but I think I'd have noticed.'

'James and I will go back and look,' Mandy offered.

They hurried back to the paddock and searched every centimetre. Then they retraced their steps back to the farmhouse, but could see no sign of the bundle of envelopes. Tom and the other farm helpers came to help search.

'This is daft!' James said. 'They *can't* have just disappeared.'

'Seems like they have,' Tom said, looking puzzled. 'I don't understand it.'

Mandy groaned. 'We'll have to do them all again.'

Tom shook his head. 'There's not time before the last post. Besides, that was the last few blank cards we had left. I'll just have to try phoning round.' He went into the farmhouse.

'It's going to take him ages,' James said. 'There were about fifty invitations.'

Mandy frowned. 'That the second time stuff's gone missing. What's going on?'

Nine

Mandy and James were relaxing in the kitchen after supper when Tom finally emerged from the farm office.

'Phew!' he said, running a hand through his sandy hair. 'I daren't think about the damage I've just done to Five Acre's phone bill! There's only one thing that's going to cheer me up.'

'Another sing-song?' Karen guessed. She was pouring a cup of tea for Pete Brady. He had stayed for supper and was relaxing before cycling home.

'Spot on!' Tom grinned round at all the helpers. No one looked too enthusiastic. 'Come on, you lot!' Tom urged. 'Make the most of this. There'll be no musical entertainment tomorrow evening – we'll be too busy getting ready for Sunday's event!'

'What a shame!' James whispered.

Mandy chuckled. 'Don't tell anyone, but I'm almost getting to enjoy these singalongs.'

James pulled a face.

As Tom went off to fetch his guitar, Pete jumped up and went after him. 'Hang on, lad. Is that old fiddle of mine still in the cupboard?'

Mandy didn't dare to look at James's face.

Pete marched back into the kitchen, proudly clutching a rather battered violin. He propped it under his chin and drew the bow across the strings. A wail that ended on a screech rose into the kitchen. 'Just needs a bit of tuning,' Pete said gruffly, twisting the wooden pegs on the instrument's neck. 'That should do it.'

He sawed at the strings and the violin gave another anguished wail.

'Sounds like a cat with its tail stuck in a door!' someone said.

As a laugh rippled round the room, Pete cleared his throat. 'Er . . . This might take a minute.'

Mandy noticed Jill watching as Pete twiddled the tuning pegs. A few moments later, another unearthly shriek seemed to tear the air apart.

Jill hurried across the kitchen. 'Having problems, Pete? Let me have a go,' she offered.

Pete looked relieved. 'I'm a bit out of practice,' he admitted, handing the fiddle over.

Mandy watched in surprise as Jill settled the violin under her chin. She made a few adjustments, nimble fingers plucking at the strings as she checked the tuning. Moments later, she drew the bow across the strings and played a string of perfect notes.

James's jaw dropped. 'I didn't know she could play!'

Mandy felt the stunned silence. 'Neither did anyone else!'

Jill went to hand the fiddle back to Pete, but he shook his head. 'Nay, lass. You seem to know what

you're doing. Why don't you play for us?'

Jill reddened. She seemed to have just realised that everyone was staring at her in astonishment. 'No. It's your violin. You play,' she said to Pete.

'Oh, go on, Jill!' someone encouraged.

'Yes,' Tom said, 'Give us a tune.'

'OK, then,' Jill murmured, with a shy smile. She closed her eyes and began to play.

The haunting notes of a classical sonata filled the kitchen. No one made a sound; the music held them spellbound. Jill played on faultlessly, swaying slightly as she put her heart and soul into her playing. When the final notes had died away, everyone cheered and clapped.

Pete Brady clapped the loudest. 'Well done, lass. That's the way my old fiddle was meant to be played!'

'That was really great,' James enthused.

'You were brilliant, Jill!' Mandy said.

Jill glanced at her, an embarrassed grin on her face. 'Thanks.'

Tom was beaming from ear to ear. 'You're a very accomplished player. Do you know any modern songs?'

'He means something he can play along to,' Karen translated.

There was a gleam in Jill's eye as she straightened

her back. 'You mean something like this?'

As Jill launched into the strains of a tune everyone recognised, Tom began strumming his guitar. Karen began to sing, and soon everyone else joined in.

For an hour or so, Jill took it in turns to play Pete's fiddle and sing.

'She's just as good at playing fun stuff,' Mandy whispered to James.

James nodded. 'She's a real star!'

'OK, everyone, time to turn in,' Karen announced, as Jill played the final notes of a song. 'Sorry to be a party pooper, but we have a lot of preparation to do tomorrow. So it'll be all hands on deck!'

'A special breakfast today for the volunteers!' Karen announced early the next morning, placing a large dish of what looked like creamy rice pudding on the table.

'What is it? Porridge?' James asked suspiciously.

Mandy stifled a giggle. She knew what James was thinking – porridge at this time of year!

'It's frumenty,' Tom said. 'A traditional recipe. Karen's thinking of selling this in the farm shop. We're her guinea-pigs! Give it a go, lad. You'll love it.' He began heaping huge, fragrant spoonfuls into his bowl.

'Er . . . right, thanks.' James helped himself to a tiny spoonful.

'It won't bite!' Karen said with a chuckle. 'It's made from our own wheat grains that have been creeing all night.'

'Creeing?' Mandy said.

'It means cooking very slowly until the grain swells. Then it's simmered with milk, fruit and spices. There's double cream in there too, courtesy of Marigold!'

James took a hesitant taste. He chewed slowly. 'This is great – all light and fluffy.'

'I'm glad you approve,' Karen said, 'because I've made an enormous batch. It's cooling in the dairy, ready to be packed into fancy jars!'

Mandy thought the frumenty was delicious. Everyone had seconds followed by grilled tomatoes on toast.

'That's one of the best things about Five Acre,' James said later, as he, Mandy and a few others went to help Pete Brady put up brightly coloured bunting and a banner reading 'Welcome to Five Acre Farm'.

'What's that?' Mandy asked.

'Karen's whopping great farm breakfasts!'

An hour or so later, the multi-coloured streamers fluttered from almost every building in the yard.

Mandy was pushing in a final drawing-pin, when a lorry and trailer pulled into the yard.

'That's the marquee,' Pete said. 'I'll go and show them where to erect it.'

'Shall we go and let the chickens out for you?' Mandy offered

'Good idea, lass,' Pete said. 'It's about the right time. Any earlier and the silly things lay their eggs all over the place. Usually in the hedges where the rats can get at them.'

Mandy and James set off. As they got close to the chicken field, Mandy stopped. 'Look!' she said, pointing to the dozens of chickens who were scratching and pecking at the grass. 'Someone's already opened the arks.'

James looked puzzled. 'But it's only you and me on chickens today.'

'Well, someone else has been over here.' She suddenly noticed that the wire mesh gate was open. 'Oh, no! Quick! If the chickens go down that track, they'll get on to the road.'

James followed her at a run. They reached the gate just as the first of the chickens began to wander out.

Mandy flapped her hands. 'Shoo!' she called. 'Shoo!'

Squawking and flapping, chickens scattered

everywhere. Mandy and James ran in circles, chasing them back inside the gate.

'Phew!' James panted, grabbing the last one. 'It's a good thing we caught them before they got run over. I wonder what silly fool left the gate open.'

'Mmm,' Mandy said, closing and latching the gate firmly. 'I wonder.' *Too many little things are going wrong lately*, she thought. And no one seemed to be responsible.

Ten

In the cowshed, Mandy had just finished washing Marigold's tail in soft soap flakes. It was early Sunday morning, the day of the fund-raising picnic. Now she was brushing it until it was smooth and silky. 'You have to look extra beautiful today,' she said. 'All sorts of people will be admiring you.'

James was brushing the cow's fawn coat until it gleamed. 'You'd never think Marigold had been sick,' he said. 'She looks fine now.'

Daniel and Jill were in Hazel's paddock. Mandy and James went across to admire the huge chestnut horse. Her coat shone. Her mane and tail had been plaited and the horse brasses on her harness gleamed. As they left the paddock, it was Jill's idea to go and sneak a quick look inside the marquee.

'Wow! Look at this!' Mandy said, in the tent's doorway. Swags and drapes of silky material lined the inside. There was a polished wooden dance floor and a stage for the band. Decorative pillars all round it had been twined with satin ribbons.

'I didn't think it was going to be so big and posh,' Daniel said, looking glum. 'My mum loves this sort of thing. I wish I'd asked Karen if she could come.'

'Why don't you go and ask her now?' James said.

'You could phone your mum,' Mandy said. 'She's coming to pick you up, isn't she? Just ask her to come earlier.'

Daniel brightened. 'Good idea! Then Mum will be able to see Copper and Comet and the piglets!' He went dashing off to find Karen.

Mandy glanced across at James. 'I hope Daniel's changed his mind about having a pet pig! And talking of pigs . . .'

When they got down to the woods, Pete doled out long-handled brushes and soapy water. 'There you go. You can give Copper and Comet a spruce-up. Ginger and Spice too – if you can catch them!'

The pigs milled about, grunting playfully, as Pete gave them a rather hit-and-miss bath. Mandy singled out Copper and Comet. She reckoned that Ginger and Spice would join in if they saw their parents enjoying a bath.

'Right. Time for your wash and brush-up!' Mandy said firmly. 'And you two had better behave!'

Copper blinked at her through his sandy lashes. Comet promptly sat down and scratched her side with a plump back leg.

'Uh-oh!' James said. 'This could prove to be difficult!'

But Copper and Comet behaved beautifully. They seemed to regard the whole bathing process as a sort of mammoth back-scratching treat. They pushed against the brushes, holding up their heads so Mandy and James could reach beneath their chins. They even stuck out their tongues to lap up the soapy water.

'Yuk!' James said. 'That must taste horrible.'

'Copper and Comet don't seem to mind!'

Ginger and Spice didn't mind either. They paddled about in the soapy water, snuffling up the suds and generally getting in the way.

Half an hour later, James put down his broom. 'Finished!'

Mandy looked at Copper and Comet, all softly glowing and with their red hair fuzzy after the bath. She creased up laughing. 'Look at these two. They look like giant day-old chicks!'

'Some really weird-looking chicks!' James spluttered.

Back at the farmhouse they ate a hurried breakfast, then went upstairs to get changed. Jill was in the bedroom. 'Have you got a minute, Mandy?' she said.

Mandy nodded, zipping up her jeans.

Jill shuffled her feet. 'You know I didn't like it here at first? Well – that was because I didn't like being pushed into coming here. But I've really loved it. It's made me less shy and I've made loads of friends . . .'

Mandy smiled. 'So – are you coming back to Five Acre Farm next year?'

Jill's face lit up in a smile. 'You bet!'

'Come on. Let's go down,' Mandy said.

Mandy and Jill met James and Daniel in the kitchen, where Karen was giving all the helpers last-minute instructions. The farm manager was wearing a pale-blue suit. Mandy thought she looked smart and efficient, with her long brown hair swept up and held with combs. 'When people start arriving,' Karen said, 'just be polite and helpful – same as you've been for the past two weeks. OK? Fingers crossed that everything goes without a hitch! I know I can count on you all.'

There were nods and smiles of agreement as

everyone dispersed. Mandy and James went out into the yard. A large white van was parked in the yard. The back doors were open and they could see that it was stacked to the roof with shelves of sumptuous flans, pies and gateaux.

'That must belong to the caterers,' James said.

Just then they saw the lanky figure of Neil Nixon walk out from behind the van. He was stuffing something down the front of his zip-up jacket. Mandy had only a brief glimpse – it looked like the plastic sprayer her mum used to mist her plants.

'What's he doing hanging round that van?' James whispered.

Before Mandy could reply, Neil saw her and James. He stopped dead. 'Er . . . Hi,' he stammered. 'I thought Karen and Tom might need an extra hand, or something . . .'

Just then, Karen came out of the farmhouse. She had a warm smile for Neil. 'Any help's much appreciated. The caterers might need a hand. Why don't you go along to the picnic field with Mandy and James and ask them?'

'Sure,' Neil said, his arms crossed tightly over his chest. 'I'll just go and take this jacket off.'

'Put it in the house if you like,' Karen said. 'Is your dad coming over later?'

'He said he would, didn't he? Dad always keeps

his word,' Neil said, defensively. He frowned. 'Why did you invite him? You know what he thinks about Five Acre Farm.'

'Your dad is entitled to his opinion,' Karen said. 'But I thought if he got to know us and saw the way we farm, it might help neighbourly relations.'

Neil looked thoughtful. 'That's fair enough, I suppose.'

'Well,' Karen said, glancing at her watch. 'Can't stand here gossiping. The band should be here by now. I wonder where they've got to.'

'Er . . . right,' Neil said hurriedly. 'I'll be back in a tick. Where's this picnic being set out?'

Neil reappeared moments later, minus his jacket. They walked past Pete Brady as they rounded the marquee. 'Hmph!' the stockman muttered, when he saw Neil with Mandy and James. 'I can't fathom why that lad's always over here. Thought he couldn't stand us lot.'

'Pete isn't too keen on me, is he?' Neil said. 'What's the grumpy old devil think I'm going to do – steal the family silver?'

Mandy flushed. 'Pete's not grumpy. Not when you get to know him.'

'No?' Neil grinned at her. His blue eyes were bright and friendly in his tanned face. 'Well, I won't be rushing to join his fan club!'

Despite herself, Mandy laughed. She thought Pete was probably right in his opinion that Neil was a chip off the old block. Neil was still prickly and defensive when anyone mentioned his father, but she reckoned he had learned a lot about the methods used on Five Acre Farm over the past two weeks.

'This looks amazing!' Mandy said. It was the first time she had seen the finished display.

Snowy cloths covered the tables in the picnic field. There were plates of tiny, fancy sandwiches, enormous savoury flans, glazed fruit tarts, pies with latticed pastry lids, gourmet dips, and even vegetables cut into decorative fish shapes, complete with sequin eyes and feathery fins. Mandy had never seen anything like them. And in the middle of it all was a splendid ice sculpture – a swan with a graceful neck and spread wings.

'It all looks good enough to eat!' James joked.

Mandy glanced towards the main gate. 'People are starting to arrive,' she said. 'I think we'd better go over there.'

For the next hour or so they welcomed local businessmen, traders and visitors, taking turns in showing them round the farm. Mandy saw Jim Nixon arrive. He looked around, stiff-necked and uncomfortable, as if he was determined not to be impressed.

Just then Mr and Mrs Hope turned up. Mandy ran forward to greet her mum and dad. They both gave her a hug and a kiss. 'Hello, love.'

'Did you enjoy your hillwalking?' Mandy asked.

Mr Hope pulled a face. 'Lovely,' he said. 'I've got blisters on my blisters!'

Mandy chuckled, then her face fell as Karen came dashing out of the farmhouse. She looked close to tears.

'Whatever's wrong?' Mrs Hope said kindly.

'I've just been on the phone,' Karen gasped. 'The band went to the wrong place. They're miles away. It could be hours before they get here!'

'But you faxed them the directions,' Mandy said. 'I saw you.'

'I know,' Karen said miserably. 'The band received another fax, at the last minute, telling them the venue had changed. Of course, when they arrived at this new venue no one had any idea what was going on. Luckily someone had the sense to phone here. The band are on their way now – but there's no telling how long they'll be.'

Mr Hope glanced at all the people making their way towards the marquee and the expected entertainment. 'I suggest we think of an alternative – and quick!'

Mandy's heart sank. After all their hard work, the day just couldn't turn into a disaster. What they needed was someone to fill in, just until the band arrived. But where were they going to find some more musicians?

'Hang on,' she said excitedly. 'I've got an idea. Tom plays guitar and Karen sings. And some of the helpers sound pretty good when they join in . . .'

'OK,' Tom said, when he'd heard her out. 'We haven't any choice. Let's give it a whirl. Mandy, can you and James round up the others? We'll meet you at the marquee.'

Mandy nodded and sped off to find James. She found him with Daniel. 'Follow me, you two!' she called and raced off across the field.

'Where to?' James panted, catching up with her.

'To find Jill,' Mandy said. 'A violinist would be the finishing touch.'

James gaped at her. 'Is it worth asking her? You know what she can be like.'

But the new, relaxed Jill was delighted to be asked. 'Course I'll help.'

James's jaw dropped. 'Wonders will never cease!' he whispered to Mandy.

Jill ran to fetch Pete's old fiddle, then returned

with it to the marquee. Karen, Tom and some of the helpers were already there waiting.

Mandy and James stood with Mr and Mrs Hope, watching from the back of the packed marquee as Karen stood up and made an announcement.

'At the last moment, we have a special addition to our programme,' she began. 'Ladies and gentlemen. For your entertainment – the Five Acre Ensemble, better known as the FAE!'

There was a polite ripple of applause. Jill tapped her bow on the edge of the violin. 'One, two, three . . .'

The music rang out in the crowded tent. It was a quirky hotch-potch, but it worked. Jill's and Karen's voices, strong and clear, pulled the sound together.

'Hey! They're pretty good,' James enthused. 'Jill's brilliant on that violin.'

When the FAE finally ran out of inspiration, there was thunderous applause and cries for more. Jill gave a signal and the fledgling band launched into an encore. Two more encores later, Karen was beginning to look strained.

But Tom signalled to her that the band had arrived. 'That's all for now, ladies and gentleman,' he announced. 'After a short internal, there will be more entertainment from the York Top Brass!'

Karen went to speak to the band leader. After the

quick exchange, the musicians began to get ready. As she came to the back of the tent, she gave a huge sigh. 'Thank goodness the roads were clear and they made better time than expected. I don't think we could have held it together for much longer.'

'We were fantastic, love!' Tom gave her a hug. 'I haven't enjoyed myself so much in ages! You can relax now. Nothing else can possibly go wrong.'

'Well, the brass band's going down a storm,' Mandy said, some time later.

'I think I preferred the FAE!' James said. 'When do you think they'll be starting on the food?'

Mandy grinned. 'Any time now I should think. The band leader has just announced that this is the last number. Shall we go outside, ready to show the guests into the picnic field?'

They walked round the side of the marquee. It was a moment before Mandy had a clear view of the adjoining field. 'Oh no!' She stood stock still, unable to believe her eyes.

The field was full of pigs. They had pulled the cloths off the tables and all the food had crashed to the floor. Now pigs trampled on snowy white cloths as they jostled for the most delicious titbits. There were pigs tucking into sandwiches, pigs smeared with expensive dips, pigs treading crushed food into the

grass. And right smack in the middle of the seething, grunting bodies were two big reddish pigs and two sturdy pink piglets.

'Copper and Comet!' Mandy groaned. 'And Ginger and Spice. Trust them!'

'Uh-oh.' James glanced behind him to where people were beginning to file out of the marquee and make their way over to the food.

Mandy's heart sank into her boots. There was no way Five Acre Farm could recover from this disaster.

Eleven

'Oh, heck!' Pete Brady groaned at Mandy's elbow. 'These two have really done it this time!' There was no doubt in his mind that Copper and Comet had been the ringleaders. He rushed towards the pigs, waving his arms about.

'Yip! Yip! Get out of there! Yip!' he cried.

Pigs ran round him squealing and grunting, grabbing a last delicious mouthful. Pete flapped his arms; he slapped at podgy bodies; he pushed at rounded rumps. Nothing made any difference. Suddenly he slipped on a squashed sandwich and sat down, right in the remains of a strawberry gateau.

'Oof!' Stunned, Pete stayed where he was.

Despite herself, Mandy felt a laugh bubbling up inside. She couldn't help it. James began to chuckle too. Even Pete saw the funny side. His weathered face lit up.

'If you can't beat 'em, join 'em!' he said, reaching for an undamaged pie. He began munching it, then suddenly his face changed. 'Ugh! Tastes horrible!'

That's odd, Mandy thought. But she had no time to consider it further. By now Tom was in the field. He wore a look of utter amazement. 'How on earth did those pigs get out? Pete's just fixed that gate!'

Karen was hard on his heels. 'Oh no! The food's ruined!'

Pete climbed slowly to his feet. Strawberries and cream were stuck to the seat of his trousers. Squashed sandwiches decorated his legs. For endless moments everyone just stood there. Then an unbelievable sound rose into the air – laughter, which got louder and louder. The elegant guests were crowding into the field, laughing as if their sides would burst.

'Look at the pigs!' someone cried.

'It's a pig's picnic!' someone else called out.

Karen looked as if she didn't know whether to laugh or cry. Just then Pete Brady came over to have a word with Tom. 'I reckon it's a good job the guests didn't eat this food,' he said.

'What do you mean?' Karen asked.

'I tasted one of those pies. It's horrible. It's been sprayed with something. Washing-up liquid, I think. Won't bother the pigs, of course!'

'But who'd do that?' Karen looked shocked. 'First the band got lost. Now this. Oh, Tom, someone's trying to sabotage our picnic!'

'Well, they won't succeed,' Tom said determinedly. He put his arm round his wife's waist. 'We're not finished yet, love. Come on!'

'Where to?' Karen said.

'The kitchen,' Tom declared. 'To rustle up some more food. You've got all that stuff put by for the farm shop and the freezer's packed with ready-cooked food.'

Mandy could see Karen's mind working. She nodded slowly. 'OK – I think we could manage that. I've a whole sack of small potatoes in the barn; pity we couldn't bake some of them . . .'

'You could,' Mandy suggested. 'If you do what Mum does. She microwaves them, then rolls them in salt and bakes them for ten minutes.'

'That's right. It works too,' Mrs Hope said, at her side, 'And I'd be happy to help out.'

Karen shot her a grateful look. 'Thanks. So – that's the food sorted. But how are we going to entertain the guests while we prepare it and get the pigs away from their feast?'

'The entertainment's easy,' Tom said. 'We'll arrange some traditional fun. How about getting our young helpers apple-bobbing? All we need is a few barrels filled with water and some apples. The guests could make pledges for who manages to get the most apples!'

'But what about the pigs?'

Mandy looked at Copper and Comet, who were still running about squealing with excitement and treading food into the grass. Ginger and Spice had chocolate cake all round their snouts. They were having the time of their lives. This was one big game to them.

'James and I can get the pigs back into their pen,' Mandy said to Tom.

James blinked at her. 'We can?'

Mandy nodded confidently. 'Remember how we got them off Nixon Manor Farm and back in their pen?'

'Oh, right,' James said. 'I get it.'

'Stick with what works, eh?' Tom grinned. 'I'll leave you and James in charge. Daniel and Jill, you're on apple-bobbing duty, OK? Come on, Karen. You and I have a date with an Aga!'

'OK,' Mandy said, once the empty buckets were lined up. 'We start gathering up the food and piling it into the buckets.'

While Mandy and James worked, and the pigs fought over the scraps, the guests watched with amusement. 'Best entertainment I've seen in years!' someone called out.

James, naturally shy, blushed to the roots of his hair. His head down, he stuffed the picnic scraps into his bucket. Soon there were only crumbs left on the grass.

'Right. Fingers crossed.' Mandy began clanging a stick against her bucket.

Copper and Comet's ears twitched. Their heads came up. This was a sound they knew and loved. Grunting with eagerness, a solid mass of boisterous pig trotted towards Mandy. The other pigs fell into line. Ginger and Spice squirmed their way to the front, tucking in behind their mother's hindquarters.

'It's working!' James breathed.

So far, so good, Mandy thought.

As she and James moved away from the ruined picnic, pigs in tow, people clapped. 'I've heard of the Pied Piper, but not the pig piper!' someone called out, setting everyone off into a fresh wave of laughter.

Mandy and James wound their way towards the woods. Heads down, black pigs, white pigs and spotted pigs trotted after Copper and Comet. The two red Tamworths ambled along, butting against each other now and then in a companionable way, their noses held high as they snuffled up the delicious smells coming from the buckets. Ginger and Spice scurried along, their short legs going all out over the grass.

Soon the guests were left behind, lured away into the farmyard, where Daniel and Jill had organised the apple-bobbing game. Tom had taken the precaution of setting out plenty of his home-brew.

'We'd better not cut through the orchard,' Mandy said, leading the way through the wheat stubble. 'Copper and Comet might be tempted to go off searching for windfalls again!'

As they approached the woods, James frowned. 'I can't work out how they escaped this time.'

'That's how – look!' Mandy pointed through the trees. Dead ahead was the fence surrounding the woods. The gate, with its pig-proof wire loop, was wide open.

'Someone let them out!' James said. 'But who?'

Mandy's blue eyes sparked with anger. 'The same person who gave the band the wrong directions and sprayed the food with washing-up liquid . . .' she began.

'You sound like you know something about it,' James said.

'I think I might . . .' And if her suspicions were correct, then the saboteur was still here at Five Acre Farm.

As Mandy and James reappeared in the farmyard there was a fresh burst of applause. Playing to the crowd, Mandy grinned. She grabbed James's sleeve. 'Come on. Take a bow!'

All around them the apple-bobbing was going down a storm, to screams of laughter and delight. The guests pledged donations for each apple plucked from the water in a helper's teeth. Even Jim Nixon had a smile on his rather stern face.

'One herd of pigs safely delivered home!' Mandy announced, coming into the kitchen.

Mrs Hope glanced over her shoulder. She had her sleeves rolled up and was rolling microwaved potatoes in salt. Mr Hope was grating cheese. He took one look at Mandy's face. 'Is something the matter, love?'

'James and I think we know who's trying to ruin the picnic,' she replied.

'Who?' asked Tom.

'Neil Nixon!' Mandy and James said together.

Karen dried her hands on a towel. 'Neil? What makes you say that?'

All eyes turned to Mandy. She felt her mouth go dry. 'Well – every time something's gone wrong, Neil's been around. I saw him coming out of Karen's office just before some important papers went missing. If he took them, he could easily have sent that last-minute fax. And he was at the paddock when Tom lost the invitations.'

She paused feeling a bit shaky.

'Go on, love,' Mr Hope said, patting Mandy's arm.

'This morning, Mandy and I saw Neil hanging about near the caterers' van,' James put in. 'He was hiding something under his jacket, wasn't he?'

Mandy nodded. 'I think it was a soap spray. So it could have been him who ruined the food. And he probably let the pigs out too. He's been down to the woods with us loads of times. And then there was the chickens . . .'

'Chickens? Hang on a minute,' Tom said. 'I agree that it looks as if Neil's responsible for some of this. But we can't just go accusing the lad . . .'

'But I know he did it!' Mandy burst out.

'Calm down, love,' Mr Hope said. 'It's all circumstantial. As they say in these TV courtroom dramas: no one actually saw Neil do anything.'

'That's right,' Karen agreed. 'I suggest we leave sorting this out until after the picnic. We've still got a hundred or more hungry guests to feed. I hate to bring money into this, but Five Acre Farm desperately needs those donations!'

'I agree,' Tom said. 'If it was Neil, he can't do any more harm. We have to salvage what we can of today. Let's keep this to ourselves for the time being.'

James nodded.

'OK,' Mandy said evenly. But inside she was boiling. She was certain she was right. And it was looking as if Neil Nixon might get away scot free!

An hour or so later, the field behind the marquee was once again buzzing with picnickers – people this time! Mandy and James helped carry out dishes of Karen's home-cooked food, taken from the freezer and heated up. There were mixed salads and mountains of tiny, crispy, baked potatoes. It had been Karen's idea to spear the potatoes on cocktail sticks.

'Like canapes,' she explained. 'There's our own butter, cheese and soured cream to go with them. And a choice of pickles and relishes. Simple but delicious.'

That certainly seemed to be the general feeling. 'Such a nice change from the usual fussy stuff these caterers serve up,' enthused a woman who seemed to be one of the sponsors. 'And all so tasty and home-grown.'

The final triumph was Karen's frumenty. Decorated with whipped cream, microwaved meringues and sugared fruit, it had become a sophisticated dessert.

'This pudding is to die for . . .' said another woman. 'You really must sell it in your new expanded farm shop.'

Mandy noticed Neil Nixon sitting by himself. He wasn't eating anything and seemed to be keeping out of the way. *As well he might*, she thought. It struck her that he was looking thoroughly miserable, but she couldn't find it in her to feel sorry for him.

Just then Jim Nixon strolled past with Tom. 'This is all your own produce?' he was saying approvingly. 'And you say this tasty butter and cheese is made in your dairy, from your own cows . . . ?'

'That's right. Let me show you our dairy . . .' Tom saw Mandy looking and winked at her.

'What's Mr Nixon talking to Tom about?' James said, appearing at Mandy's side.

'Would you believe – traditional farming methods and Five Acre Farm's tasty food?'

James's jaw dropped. 'Cripes!'

Mandy grinned. 'I couldn't believe it either!'

In fact, Jim Nixon seemed so interested in having

the grand tour of Five Acre Farm that he was one of the last guests to leave. Mandy and James saw him going into the farmhouse with Tom.

Mandy hadn't seen Neil for some time. 'I wonder where he is,' she said to James. 'Do you think he's feeling guilty?'

'Huh! He jolly well should be!' James said. Like Mandy, he was in no doubt as to who was the saboteur. 'Shall we go inside? My feet are killing me!'

Mandy nodded. It was almost reckoning time for Neil. Sympathy for him was beginning to creep in. Despite everything, she didn't think he was all bad.

'But that's amazingly generous of you!' they heard Karen saying as they came into the kitchen. She was talking to a pleasant, round-faced woman, who introduced herself as Daniel's mum. No one had noticed her arrive in all the excitement.

'I'm only too pleased to donate to such a good cause.' Mrs Shaw handed over a cheque. 'Daniel's gained so much from being here. I've a feeling we might be looking into pigs. I've been thinking of having the garden landscaped and I think we could spare a half acre!'

Mandy couldn't believe her ears. 'She must have pots of money!' she hissed to James.

James chuckled. 'So Daniel might get to have a pet pig, after all!'

Karen seemed overwhelmed. 'People have donated far more money than we'd expected. There's enough to keep the farm going *and* pay for extending the shop.'

'That's brilliant, love!' Tom gave his wife a hug. 'Your food clinched it. I always said that you didn't need to hire caterers!'

'Maybe I'll listen to you next time!' Karen said with a twinkle. 'But I can't promise anything! Now who's for a cup of tea?'

Mr and Mrs Hope were in the kitchen along with Jill, Daniel and his mum, and the Capthornes. Jim Nixon sat at the kitchen table, deep in conversation with Pete Brady. 'So you're saying that organic methods can be used alongside the more usual farming practices?' Jim commented.

'Looks like there could be a truce between Five Acre and Nixon Manor,' James whispered to Mandy.

Suddenly a lanky, dark-haired figure blundered into the kitchen. Neil's face was set and there was a pale line round his mouth.

'Neil!' Jim Nixon said. 'I was wondering where you'd sloped off to. Come and sit down, lad. I was just talking to Pete here . . .'

'I've got something to say to Karen and Tom first,' Neil burst out. He swallowed nervously as everyone turned to look at him.

'Go on then, son,' Jim ordered, not unkindly. 'Spit it out.'

Neil chewed at his bottom lip. Mandy thought she knew what he was about to say. Her stomach tightened for him.

'It was me,' Neil said in a low voice. 'I faxed the band. I sprayed washing-up liquid on the food. I let the pigs out. And all the other stuff – the milk that got wasted, the papers that went missing, the invitations, the chickens – that was me too.'

Jim Nixon's eyebrows shot up into his hair. 'But why? What the dickens got into you . . . ?' He started to get to his feet, but Tom laid a hand on his arm.

'Let's hear the lad out, Mr Nixon,' Tom said calmly.

Mandy saw that everyone had stopped talking and begun to listen. Poor Neil was red to his ears.

'Why did you do it, Neil?' Karen seemed concerned for the miserable lad. 'I thought you enjoyed coming over to Five Acre. You seemed to be really interested in our methods.'

'I did and I am,' Neil said in a wavery voice. 'But I had Nixon Manor to think about. Dad was always going on about how it would be better for us if you packed up and shipped out. Then Five Acre Farm might get run properly.'

'That's true enough,' Jim admitted, looking

sheepish. 'I believe in speaking my mind. But I've never encouraged Neil to do anything unlawful!'

'I know.' Neil hung his head. 'It was all my idea to make it look as if Five Acre was inefficient and sloppy, so then the sponsors wouldn't want to donate any more money. Only – I started to get really interested in organic farming and it got harder and harder to keep on messing things up for Karen and Tom. I kept pushing myself into it – even though it felt wrong. I'm sorry for what I tried to do. Really sorry. And I'm sorry I've let you down too, Dad.'

Mandy could see that Neil must have had a real struggle with himself. It couldn't have been easy for him, having a father he looked up to – but didn't agree with.

Jim jumped up and faced his son. He seemed more confused than angry. 'Why didn't you come and talk to me about this change of heart?'

Mandy saw Neil shrug. He stood there all skinny and sharp angles, as stubborn as his dad in his own way. 'I thought you'd go wild. Organic is a dirty word in our house.'

'It might surprise you to learn that I'm changing my own opinions about Five Acre Farm's methods. Live and let live might be the best policy from now on.'

'Huh?' Neil gulped. 'But you never admit to being

wrong about anything...' He broke off, embarrassed.

Jim Nixon's mouth dropped open. Then he gave a gruff laugh. 'Aye, well. Maybe I asked for that!' He turned to Tom and Karen. 'I take full responsibility for my son. I'll pay for the damage and for the extra food. If it's all right with you, we'll be going now.' His face hardened. 'You needn't worry that Neil's going to get away with this. He's done wrong and he's got to be made to realise that.'

By the look on Jim Nixon's face, Neil was going to be grounded for a year, Mandy thought. She racked her brains, trying to think of a way to help him.

Tom stepped forward. 'Hold on a minute. I reckon Neil deserves some credit for facing us all like this. I'm not making excuses for what he's done. It was stupid and thoughtless, but there's no real harm done. Karen and I are willing to forgive and forget, aren't we, love?'

Karen nodded. 'I think you might go a bit easy on the lad.'

'No offence, but I'll deal with my son the way I see fit,' Jim Nixon said coldly. 'The Nixons pay their dues. Always have. Right, Neil?'

All the fight seemed to have gone out of Neil now. He nodded miserably, big bony hands hanging by his sides. 'Yeah. Right, Dad.'

Suddenly, Mandy had the perfect idea. She took her courage in both hands and spoke up politely. 'Mr Nixon? Can I make a suggestion? What if there was some way Neil could make amends . . . ?

The late afternoon was glorious at Five Acre. Mandy and James waved as the cars carrying the last of the helpers moved away. Daniel hung out of one window. 'See you next year,' he called.

'Bye, Daniel,' Mandy and James called. 'Bye,' they called to Jill, as she waved from a back window. 'Take care!'

'It's about time we made tracks too, love,' Mr

Hope said, when the cars had disappeared.

'Can we just go and say goodbye to Copper and Comet?' Mandy pleaded.

Mr Hope chuckled. 'Course you can. I've a feeling you might find someone else with them already.'

Mandy and James looked at each other. They had that feeling too!

Down at the woods, they saw two figures leaning on the wooden fence – Pete Brady, back in his usual blue overalls and cloth cap, and Neil Nixon. They went and stood next to them.

The deep orange sun cast a glow through the trees, making Copper and Comet's hairy coats look even more fiery. Ginger and Spice were stretched out, sleeping off the effects of their stolen picnic.

Neil reached over to scratch Copper's back with a sturdy stick. 'You like that don't you, you old rascal?'

Copper made a happy snorting sound and grinned up at Mandy and James.

'I'm really going to miss these two and their babies,' Mandy sighed.

'Yeah? Not for long though,' Neil said. 'You'll have all those other animals to look after at Animal Ark.'

Mandy nodded. That was true. But Copper and Comet would always have a special place in her heart.

'Besides,' Neil said. 'I'll make sure these bruisers get plenty of attention.'

'Will you bring the pig bucket down for them every night?' James asked.

Neil grinned, blue eyes bright under his mop of dark hair. 'You bet – since I'm going to be coming here pretty often! Pete says he'll turn me into an expert on organic pig farming in no time.'

Pete winked at Mandy. He had surprised everyone by agreeing to Mandy's suggestion that Neil could make amends by working on Five Acre in his spare time.

'Some punishment!' James said. 'Getting to know Copper and Comet!'

'Terrible, isn't it?' Neil agreed with a wide grin. He glanced at Mandy. 'Thanks for everything. This means a lot to me.'

'Oh, that's OK,' Mandy replied. She always got embarrassed when people thanked her.

'Why don't you tell Mandy and James your news, Neil?' Pete prompted.

Neil's mouth stretched in a grin that reached from ear to ear. 'Dad's agreed to let me keep a few rare breeds. Karen's agreed to sell us Copper and Comet's next lot of babies. And I'm going to rear them organically.'

'Oh,' Mandy said, her eyes shining. 'That's fantastic!'

'It sure is!' James said.

Mandy leaned over to give Copper and Comet a final scratch. Suddenly Comet launched herself at Copper. She gave his ear a play bite, then streaked off up the field, inviting him to pursue her. Copper squealed loudly. He wheeled round and dashed after his mate, trotters flying over the grass.

'Go, Comet!' Mandy said. 'Copper'll never catch you!'

She gave a chuckle. With these two around, Neil was going to have his work cut out!

TABBY IN THE TUB
Animal Ark 41

Lucy Daniels

Mandy Hope loves animals more than anything else. She knows quite a lot about them too: both her parents are vets and Mandy helps out in their surgery, Animal Ark.

A feral tabby cat has turned up in Welford and Mandy is worried. The poor thing is about to have kittens and she has no one to look after her. Bill Ward, the postman, comes to the rescue, allowing the tabby to make herself at home in his garden shed. And, before long, the tabby is able to return the favour in a very special way . . .

ANIMAL ACTION

If you like *Animal Ark* then you'll love the RSPCA's Animal Action Club! Anyone aged 13 or under can become a member for just £5.50 a year. Join up and you can look forward to six issues of Animal Action magazine - each one is bursting with animal news, competitions, features, posters and celebrity interviews. Plus we'll send you a fantastic joining pack too!

To be really animal-friendly just complete the form – a photocopy is fine – and send it, with a cheque or postal order for £5.50  (made payable to the RSPCA), to Animal Action Club, RSPCA, Causeway, Horsham, West Sussex RH12 1HG. We'll then send you a joining pack and your first copy of *Animal Action.*

Registered charity no 219099

Don't delay, join today!

Name ....

Address ....

....

Postcode ....

Date of birth ....

Youth membership of the Royal Society for the Prevention of Cruelty to Animals

AACHOD2

PIGS AT THE PICNIC

Mandy and James had just entered the woods when Daniel and Jill came running towards them.

'Now what?' Mandy groaned.

'We can't find Copper and Comet,' Daniel panted.

'Or the piglets!' Jill said.

Mandy was already dashing through the trees, James at her heels. As they drew close to the pen, there was an unnerving silence.

Mandy moved round the outside wall, an inkling of what had happened forming in her mind. She saw the wooden posts all askew, and a sheet of corrugated iron bent up at the corner. There were a few ginger coloured hairs attached to the edge of the metal sheet.

'They've escaped,' she announced. 'We've *got* to find them!'

'Er . . . I think we already have. Look!' James pointed through the trees.

Two large reddish shapes and two small pink blobs were making their way along the edge of Jim Nixon's wheatfield.

Mandy's eyes widened in horror. 'Oh, heck,' she moaned. 'We're going to need help. If they get into that cornfield they'll be in big trouble!'

Animal Ark series